THE STANDARD OF PITCH IN RELIGION

THE STANDARD
OF
PITCH IN RELIGION

BY

THOMAS ARTHUR SMOOT, D.D.

WILDSIDE PRESS

Dedication

To the memories of the Reverend James
Franklin Smoot and his Wife, Virginia
Brittingham, whose lives, by the
standard called Christian,
were pitched according
to the norm

CONTENTS

CONTENTS

THE STANDARD OF PITCH IN RELIGION

Chapter I

FUNDAMENTALS AND OVERTONES

AS the taut string has its fundamental note, upon which the whole musical gamut is based, so human life must have its fundamental, which becomes a determining factor in all conduct and activities. It is useless to ask which are more essential to the excellency of the musical instrument, its primary or its secondary tones: both are indispensable. Equally empty would be the question, Which is the more important, the cardinal principle of one's life or an irradiation from that principle? Or, Which are the essential elements in success, fundamentals or reduced principles of conduct? We might as pertinently inquire, Which is more necessary, the foundation of a house or the house?

Every life is an entity of complex relationships. We find the utmost difficulty in analyzing ourselves. When we fancy that we have found a ruling motive somewhere in the vast labyrinths of the soul, we are sure to discover sometime later on, if we search diligently, that other motives overlap and give color to what we fain would call the simple basis. And yet, this very fact gives to human life much of its zest and sweetness.

If one could find a stringed instrument which produced only fundamental tones, one would have a dull time of it in making music. The monotonous humdrum would cause pain, not pleasure. Such an instrument is an impossibility in the realms of music; but it is sadly true that there are some soul instruments in the realm of spiritual music that have lost their quality; in which certain soft, sweet overtones are lacking. Nobody is eager to hear such a heart give forth its empty sounds. The delicate and gentle, the tender and the compassionate have faded out of life. There may be the fundamental note of honesty, or money, or pleasure: be that as it may; let the isolated aim and purpose spring out of a motive indifferent, fair, or good, and the world turns away from the monotonous thrumming. For if one's sole virtue is even so good a principle as honesty, accompanied by no kindness or compassion, one can not be very attractive to those in need. Some of the most miserly, unfeeling souls that I have ever known were those that thrummed forever on the one string of honesty. And this I say despite the fact that the world is so sadly in need of a more rigid type of honesty in all walks of life. We need not even pause to note the utter vapidness of the sound that grates forth from such gross fundamentals as love of money or love of pleasure.

Likewise, if one could find a stringed instrument that gave forth nothing but overtones, one would be put to it to make any music, since the basis of pitch would be lacking. There might be a certain combination of sweetness, but the tones would run wild with no governor to restrain them. There could be no such instrument of music; but there are some soul-instruments that seem to be constructed upon so unfortunate a basis. Some, we find, have certain redeeming traits; but, lacking in the great essentials of character, their lives are well-nigh worthless to humanity. A man is dissipated, dishonest, indolent, and yet may show kindness to a dog; a woman is selfish, flippant, envious, but kisses away the tears from a waif's face for love's sake. The overtones from such souls are sweet, if we could isolate them long enough to get their full flavor. But how beautiful, indeed, would they be, if blended into a symphony of a genuinely manly or womanly life!

And this last statement leads me to dwell upon one of the most important achievements in life, *viz.*, finding those sweet overtones in lives where chaos reigns, and making them stand out with a firmness and distinctness that shall turn them into fundamentals. There is a standard, a norm in our social, moral and religious life, just as there is a standard pitch in music. And as notes are dependent upon a varying pitch, reached by successive, graded steps above the standard, so are there different grades or planes of conduct among men, and what may seem but an overtone to one, may appear as a fundamental to another.

To revert to the example given above, the norm in society does not lead to any concern about a stray dog, and yet the kindness of the outcast to that unfortunate animal may be a fundamental, an octave higher than the standard pitch of the human heart. The unlikeable woman who kissed away the tears from the child's face, might find her "fundamental" in an orphan's home, where, becoming interested in the fatherless ones, all of the pent-up notes of sweetness in her soul might burst forth into a song of helpfulness to the world.

Von Helmholtz invented a resonator, which, when held to the ear, selects a tone of certain pitch and intensifies it so that it may be heard distinctly above other tones of differing wave lengths. By means of a series of resonators, the deep tones lying beneath the auditory range, may be "pulled up," so to speak, to the plane of hearing, while the short sound-waves, playing above the auditory range, may be "pulled down" to the hearing plane. Hence, it is quite evident that there are many sound-waves in action all around us which we do not recognize because of our limitations in hearing ability.

Analogously, there is much of the sweet music of the human heart being lost because nobody hears it. There are stray tones floating about in low places and high, which might come in to make a chord in the world's grandest symphony, if some skilled musician would step in long enough to hold the resonator to a sympathetic ear.

A grave fault in human nature is that we are prone to train ourselves to appreciate only that music which is based on our own fundamentals. Any other pitch is lost on us because we have no other means of transforming it into the same wave lengths of our own tones. The increase in the range of our musical soul-gamut is a laudable purpose for every man. The whole world appreciates the high-grade man, with his wisdom and knowledge, his fine soul and character; but the man beneath the norm, whose life is on a low plane, gets little attention or care. Anybody can admire the character of lovely Agnes, looking down upon her David Copperfield, like an inspiring angel; but there is something in the life of the "child-wife," too, that the world needs and can admire, if it be no more than the plaintive, dying note, "It is better as it is." Even Micawber has some place in the world's symphony. Dickens knew how to sweep the "harp of a thousand strings," and blend myriads of differing notes into a harmonious concordance. There was sweetness in the life of Paul and Florence Dombey; anybody could detect that. But how about Cap'n Cuttle, and the proud Mr. Dombey? There was something there, too, and trained, skilled fingers could bring it out. But the world, generally speaking, would pass by both of these characters and stamp them as being not worth the outlay of one's time to investigate.

Some day, let us believe, the stock of resonators is going to be so increased that every man will deem a set of them necessary to his equipment in life, and will be listening to stray chords and notes from human souls that have in some way lost their places in the song of creation and redemption.

It needs further to be said that a good deal of sweetness is being lost out of really well-ordered lives, possessing a good fundamental tone, with some helpful chords emanating therefrom. Some lives are careless of the overtones here and there that have their places of helpfulness, which have become a negligible factor to these life-players. A good man may mar the symphony of his life by the discordant overtone arising out of envy. I have known that one despicable overtone to ruin an otherwise great song. And what might I say of hate, malice, pride—overtones that have become the source of discord to so many songs of life? What a pity that these minor tones should neutralize the effect of a splendid aggregation of fine fundamentals! "He is an excellent man, but he has one fault," is the comment heard now and again. The fault is not irremediable; no man has a right to resign himself to that thought; for there is an eternal behest, running through nature, urging all things toward perfection. Man is no exception to nature's rule.

Rectifying the harp of life, installing a new set of resonators, gathering up the stray tones out of the lives of others and retuning the ill-strung instrument in our own hands—these are tasks that belong to us. To learn the value of small things, to appreciate the atom as being part of the boulder, to learn that the vocabulary of childhood is indispensable to the understanding of a world-language—these are objects of knowledge worthy any man's time to acquire.

The fundamental things in life are never too big or important not to be attended by some essential, tho small and subsidiary things. So long as even a minor detail is wrong in the government of the soul, there is a lofty aim before the soul— the removal or rectification of the wrong.

The world needs every great river and ocean; but it can not afford to lose one drop of water. What effect it would have on this universe, if one of its atoms should be annihilated, I am not wise enough even to fancy; but this I know: it is impossible to bring about such a complete destruction of this invisible portion of matter, and therefore, its conservation on the part of the Creator must be essential to His plans and purposes concerning the cosmos. If this be true concerning matter, how eminently true it must be of spirit!

As the material world needs its every atom and water-drop and fleck of gold, so the human race is in need of every man, and every faculty of every man, embracing each minor emotion and thought.

The fundamental tone of the soul needs to be clear and sweet; but the overtone must be just as true in order to blend with the "music of the spheres." The soul that can reach an octave higher or lower than its own normal pitch will be invited to sing with archangels.

The question of standard pitch thrusts itself upon us, demanding, How can we avoid confusion and clang of sound in a world where myriads of temperaments would seem to call for innumerable fundamentals? Would not a multiplicity of fundamentals, differing in wave-lengths, destroy the harmony of the symphony of the human race? The reply reminds us, that in the musical world there is an international standard of pitch, agreed upon by instrument-makers, which calls for uniformity of basic tone. By this agreement, a piano made in France has the same quantitative value, as to physical wave-lengths, in its fundamental tones, as a piano made in America.

And in reality, this agreement of the makers of instruments goes back for its authority to common and inherent principles of the human race, without regard to language, color or culture. For it is a well-known fact that savages in the jungles of the Amazon River have been known to weep under the charm of a violin, from which a missionary drew the sweet melody of "Jesus, Lover of My Soul." These wild men of the forest, fierce children of nature, had their javelins uplifted to thrust through the white intruder; but when he began to sing, and drew his bow tremulously in tender accompaniment, the hard hearts of the natives melted, their arms were grounded, and tears of compassion streamed down their swarthy faces. They did not know a word that was sung; the theme of the hymn was a blank to them; of music as a science they were totally ignorant; but their hearts were set to the standard pitch of humanity, and they caught the melody, understood its language, and yielded to its thrilling story.

If there is surely a uniform standard of pitch in the musical world, based upon physical qualities of a common sensory nervous system, as well as a certain similarity of mental activity, just as truly there exists the norm of moral conduct in the arena of racial activities. There must be some standard pitch by which harmony is to be determined and measured in the world. There is not one standard for white, another for black people; all must yield to the authority of a common fundamental.

It is in keeping with this logical principle of human existence that Jesus of Nazareth became the norm of human life, the fundamental tone for all moral conduct, the standard of pitch for all time and for all men as pertains to morals and religion. We should of necessity have great confusion in the world of moral action but for this law, exemplified by the Founder of Christianity. What might be deemed right in England would be condemned as wrong in the United States; the morals of China would be incompatible with those of Africa, under the negation of the truth in question. The world could never get together on anything of moral value. Definition itself would become misty, since terms for honesty and purity in one country would be invalid and inoperative in another.

Quite naturally, then, the Son of Man, with acute understanding of the entire race, declared that He was the Way, the Truth, and the Life. That is, He was the norm of right conduct; His life was to be the standard of pitch of all activities among men—social, moral, religious. Nor does the truth of this declaration in any sense affect the autonomy of any mortal, or limit the range of his achievements. A piano under the touch of a master has the same fundamental as it does under the touch of a novice, but the performances of the two differ as much as do day and night. More, even the master may continuously become more skilled, learn new combinations, and widen the range of his accomplishments. It is equally true that in establishing a norm of conduct within Himself, the Son of Man was only proceeding along the highway of the essential truth, that in God's universe there must be unity and harmony, whether it be in the physical or moral sphere.

The revolutionary value of Jesus of Nazareth in the world, both morally and physically, must have a profound recognition in any philosophy of life that looks for a sane and single standard of conduct. Without such a standard the various systems of ethics remind us of the "sounding brass and tinkling cymbal." The principle of unity set forth in the Christian system declares as its ultimate objective the correlation of any and all forces whatsoever, looking toward an eternal conquest in the interest of the truth. But just as the fundamental tone of an instrument has its myriads of overtones, with innumerable combinations, capable of being extended to infinity, so does the everlasting standard of pitch established by the Son of Man connote for humanity a vastness of range in effort, a breadth of vision, and a glory of attainment that stagger the potential possessors with responsibility.

Chapter II

THE GREATNESS OF MIND

IF the analogies between matter and mind that have been presented in the preceding chapter are in any large sense worthy of credence, humanity needs to stop still and, looking within its own heart, take an inventory of its possibilities. I say inventory; and yet, such can not be done in the full sense, for that would imply a complete appraisal of man's resources. And this can never be attained. The task is beyond the range of human calculus. The fundamental note of humanity as established by Jesus of Nazareth connotes an infinitude of overtones that tend to swell into every nook and cranny of an unlimited universe. To express it by yet another figure, *man,* as defined in terms of the Son of Man, must have as his exponent a term whose function is not completed until it has been lifted to the nth power.

There came to me recently an opportunity to illustrate the greatness of the mind with which man is endowed. While buying papers at a news-stand, I observed a keen-eyed little Russian Jewess peering around my elbow, evidently intent upon arresting attention. "I heard you talk at the opening exercises of school yesterday morning," she remarked, with a glow of interest upon her face. "And what did I say, my little girl?" was my query. "You said that our heads were bigger than the United States, and that our hearts were large enough to cover the continent," she replied, with a triumphant smile. "I went home and told father about it," she continued, "and he said he suspected it was pretty nearly true."

I was pleased to see that my address to the school children had borne some fruit, if in no other mind than that of this obscure child, to whom there had come a fresh gleam of light as to her potentialities. In truth, our heads—which means our hearts, too—are larger than our great country, in a distinctive sense, and we shall never have done exploiting their untold resources, if we but keep at the task, in faith and hope. The nations of the world have partitioned up the earth with such greedy care that all is now taken; no discoverer may add to his country's possessions by opening up new territory in the future. But we individual men and women can fit out exploring expeditions into the vast world of mind, and find new continents, oceans, and islands of thought. One admires the spirit of that ancient hero of Trojan wars and later wanderings, who, in one of Tennyson's fine poems, exhorts his old mariners, after their return home:

> " . . . Come, my friends,
> 'Tis not too late to seek a newer world.
> Push off, and sitting well in order smite
> The sounding furrows; for my purpose holds
> To sail beyond the sunset, and the baths
> Of all the western stars, until I die."

He is not content to recline in ease and idleness; that could bring no pleasure to such a spirit as his. But,

> "To strive, to seek, to find, and not to yield,"

seems to him a joy worthy of being an end within itself for the earth-born mortal.

The psychologist assures us that there are between six hundred million and two billion cells in the human brain. It must follow that the combinations possible for so vast a number are well-nigh infinite. And since memory, the prerequisite of all knowledge, is dependent upon cell-changes, it must be concluded that the mind, working through the brain, is practically without limit as to its possibilities of acquirement of facts and truths. "The wisest person that ever lived probably had several million brain-cells that were more or less idle." To demonstrate the truth of these statements graphically, take the number, one hundred, and interest yourself by observing the many combinations you may make from it. Then, having grown weary with so small a task as that, reflect upon the extent to which you can form new aggregations of brain-cells out of the two billion that are at your disposal! And every such aggregation of cells gives a new point of vision as to the mind's glory and extent.

The formation of these new thought-centers may be compared to the turning of a kaleido-scope, by which new configurations are brought before the eye. The static mind, in like manner, may have wonderfully beautiful pictures before it, but unless the machine revolves, no new scenes appear. The difference between the static, and therefore empty, mind, and the active, aggressive mind, may be illustrated by the contrast between the sluggard in his rags and the industrious, pros-perous citizen and man of affairs, dwelling in plenty, which becomes more abundant auto-matically.

The mind has a superficial vastness that we might compare to the topography of the earth. If one man were to endeavor to visit every continent of the earth, and every island of the seas, to explore every mountain to its topmost crag and every river to its smallest tributary, he would have covered the whole planet in less time than he could have as minutely traversed the periphery of the human brain, with all of its potentialities for thinking. And having in a cycle traversed the brain once, he might cover it again and again a thousand times, and even in his final journey he would observe new objects of truth and beauty, just as the traveler around the globe finds new scenes of inspiration and joy.

But there is a world beneath the surface, more wonderful in the mind than in the earth. We are continuously sinking shafts into the mines for treasures and wonders hidden underneath the crust of our planet, and man will never, to the end of time, be able to exploit them all. Much less shall we ever be able to bring out all of the hidden wealth that lies buried beneath the surfaces of our own hearts. The deeper we go, the richer are the discovered treasures. If you sink a shaft into the mine of science, you can never work it to a finish; if you go into the mine of philosophy, its treasures are endless. So of all branches of human knowledge.

If men but realized the wealth that lies hidden within themselves, but *realized* it, I repeat, there would be no idleness, no wasted years, no vicious habits. For to realize means to make actual in consciousness as a fact or entity; and no man, while laying hold of the richest jewels of the human soul, would or could let them drop in idleness, nor could he walk off indifferently and leave them, in order to gather up germ-filled garbage out of the world's trash-pile.

A man needs only to "come to himself" in order to become better. The slave of passion groans at times of divine illumination, craving to be delivered from the bondage of bad habit. And yet, if men but realized it, the baser passions die easily when the soul climbs into the higher realms of thought. It is easy to lop off bad habits in the wonderful world of mind. The cure for hurtful impulses lies, not in fighting them, but rather in going away and leaving them. A sensuous soul can battle against its desires by the hour and be none the better for the conflict, while an excursion, in company with some master-mind into the realms of spirit, causes the soul to forget the lower passions, and so rescues the life from destruction. A strong book has made many a long winter's evening short, and thereby turned the dross of many a soul, by a wondrous process of alchemy, into pure gold.

The mind itself never wears out. As long as the brain-tissue remains unimpaired the mind can continue to use it for as good work as was ever done. The hands and feet grow feeble, the eyes and ears lose their powers, but the mind itself never grows weary nor impotent. It is the only part of us that grows brighter and stronger with age and use. And this is true because it is the only infinite thing about us, the very essence of undying selfhood. I could think of mind in no other way with any degree of satisfaction to myself. If it wears out like the body, then mind in its essence is painfully powerless, not to be entrusted with the vital issues of the universe. Indeed, if mind-decay were possible, our possessions would all be delusive unrealities.

I am aware that impaired brain-tissue cuts off the mind's power of demonstrating itself here in the material world; this must be admitted. But until that time comes the mind moves on, an example of perpetual motion. The more it gives out the more is left. "He that saveth his life shall lose it, and whosoever loseth his life, for

My sake (*i.e.*, the sake of the Great Mind of the universe) shall find it." The man that is sparing with his thought shall die poor, and whosoever is lavish in its use shall be rich by reason of his prodigality.

Some men are really stingy with their thoughts, and it naturally follows that they themselves should come to want. If "the liberal soul shall be made fat," it is well to give out the very best mental product one has at all times. Economy in a household is fine wisdom with every thing except thought, and that commodity should be lavishly used at all times. Often we act as tho we considered any substitute for the highest thought as being good enough for home consumption. But such parsimony will cost alarmingly in the end by producing leanness of soul. The woman who opened her house to Elijah had enough food for her needs, altho she scraped the bottom of the barrel every day, and poured out the last drop of oil as well. She and her guest had faith. In like manner, we should dip out enough mental pabulum to serve for a full dinner, even tho we scrape the bottom in order to do it. If one gives freely, one must ever receive freely. He that goes to the bottom of the barrel for the last handful of meal will find more when he returns, and whoever empties his cruse of oil into the cup of his hungry fellow, is sure to find his vessel filled when he takes it up again.

Taking this view of mental activity, it becomes easily apparent that the faculty for thinking indicates a high form of religious duty. Moreover, religion becomes a central fact in the highest forms of mentality, so that all thought is literally governed by the fundamental note, religion, which means attitude toward God. The Pauline injunction, "Let this mind be in you, which was also in Christ Jesus," passes over to us for consideration the superb proposition that a man may become so completely saturated with the love of Christ that the output of his mind will be a reproduction of the thought of Christ. He thinks in the terms of the Being who redeemed him, made him anew; caused him to become reborn, and in a marvelously true sense to have the imprimatur of his Father stamped upon him.

Only upon an hypothesis of the unlimited range of the mind in its final reaches can man with any intelligent effort undertake to work out a destiny that sweeps beyond the borders of time. Granted his survival after the death of the body, and we have before us the widest range of prophetic outlook as to what shall befall the soul through eternity. And yet I must have some precursor in that unknown world in order to steady my faith and give me the assurance of hope. This want of my heart is met in the person of Jesus Christ, whose declaration of his mission as forerunner localizes the soul's objective in the "Father's house." This personal touch warms the human heart and removes from the mind a certain fear of the other world that would otherwise make it ghost-like and uncanny. Moreover, an apostle who was close to his Master before and after death, said: "We know that when He shall appear, we shall be like Him." In the light of such assurance the trusting mind learns to contemplate crossing the borders of time with a degree of complacency, which even grows into eager expectation.

Chapter III

THE FRIENDLY ATTITUDE

SUCH a view of the human mind suggests to any reflecting individual a concept of life that embraces as a field of operation the entire universe, material and spiritual. If the soul has had its habitat upon this planet, and with a measure of success wrought out its destiny here, amid warring forces, it is possible to conceive of the entire universe as being an expanded sphere for continued soul-activities. Such a fact would furthermore place upon the human mind a tremendous responsibility, namely, that of properly equating life on this side of death with the life beyond the great divide. Too much attention of a certain type to earthly affairs crowds into one part of the equation certain extraneous factors that have no counterpart on the eternal side. Equally true may be the statement that some over-spirituelle persons might give a fictitious value to the equation on the thither side of life, rendering necessary the introduction of false entries on the hither side of the equation, thus making human existence fanciful, mystical and impractical.

The question logically arising in the well ordered human mind at this point is, What should be my attitude toward the present material world in which I live? What is my relation to matter from an ethical and religious viewpoint? Does the material base of my existence affect in any essential sense my soul-motives, both as to this life and the life extended beyond? These, and many other questions hammer at the door of reason for admission into the council chamber of conscience, where all problems of an ethical character must be solved. For, whatever may be our philosophy of life, the fact of evil is linked to the fact of materiality, just as indissolubly as is the fact of good. An essential connection in our experience between matter and ethics renders our attitude toward matter a subject of paramount importance.

For I must have an attitude of friendliness or hostility; of indifference or interest; of joy or sorrow; of hope or despair. It is quite possible for me to look upon the earth as a low-ground of sorrow, filled with weeping willows, upon which anon I may hang my harp, having refused to sing or rejoice. I can look upon the world, so constituted, as being filled with enmity toward me, and hostile to my final happiness and welfare. And so, I may assume the attitude of hostility toward all my surroundings. In contradistinction to this attitude, I may enter upon my career with a feeling of friendliness toward the material of this present world, its laws, forces, and warring elements. It is my privilege to hold out the hand of friendship to the forces of nature, and even tho I may feel the prick of thorns and briers for my trouble, I can bind up the wounds, assuring myself with a smile that I have tried to shake hands in the wrong way; that nature's heart is essentially good and kind, and that she will at last give me a friendly grip.

It is only by meeting the great world of our human kind in such a spirit, that we may hope to have friends. The surly individual offers no market for friendship, and hence, rarely has any in stock. There are times when he would like to possess some of the commodity, but his parsimonious expenditure of effort has rendered it improbable that he should have it. Friendship is a fair spirit who rejoices to make her abode in the sunny gardens where open roses with the morning dew upon them. She can not live in dark places nor cellars where flourish fungous plants; friendship droops and dies among molds, mildews, and mushrooms.

And this attitude of friendliness is the basis for the possession of friends, not only in the human world, but in every other. The student must be friendly toward his books or they will never "warm up" to him. The geologist must be friendly toward the rocks if he would have them tell their secrets; the chemist must look most kindly upon dark precipitates and biting acids if he would coax out of them a true story of their combining powers. Often have I seen a youth make a lasting enemy of mathematics merely because he began the ugly habit of frowning upon arithmetic, snarling at algebra, and later on casting defamatory aspersions upon the good character of geometry. He may even have torn leaves from a treatise on that science, or flung the book harshly and disrespectfully upon the floor in his wrath against an unoffending presentation of the truth. Is it any wonder that the science assumed a hard and unapproachable attitude toward him, and kept it up until, for good and all, the two parted company?

The friendly attitude toward life, in its broad and all-inclusive sense, is certainly better than the unfriendly viewpoint. By such a spirit of friendliness one gets more out of living, and leaves a larger contribution to the world in the end. The martial attitude may have been necessary in early days, involving the setting up of tribe against tribe, and the destruction of property and life, but one can not help picturing in the mind the ideal world we might have now if warfare had ceased several centuries ago. What splendid energies have run to waste in the streams of blood that have flown upon ten thousand battle-fields on the plains of Europe and America! How much priceless treasure, the concrete expression of the hard toil of men, has gone up in smoke through warfare, thus lowering the world's efficiency!

"But is not life within itself a struggle, and must not every organism fight in order to live?" Yes; but let the fight be a friendly one. A good-natured day-laborer is more effective in the end than one that is ill-natured. The manufacturer that feels happy and looks bright can make a better cloth than his competitor that is angry with him. The banker that curbs his temper and looks pleasant can count money more accurately than the surly man at his side who has lost his temper. Your business man that goes frowning and snorting down to the arena of trade is in good frame to "knock down and drag out" all opponents, from a physical standpoint, but on a mental basis, which is the real one, he is far weaker to hold his own than if he were in good humor. And even in a physical contest, which may sometimes be thrust upon one, the too tense nerve and muscle often means defeat. The Japanese system of wrestling called jiu-jitsu owes its effectiveness to the non-resistive attitude of the body to that of its antagonist. The master in this art trains his body to yield, bend, recoil, in such fashion as to cause his opponent to dislocate his own limbs and joints by the very fierceness of the attack which he himself makes. The wrestler in this system utilizes his antagonist's strength by causing it to expend itself against a constantly receding object, the effect of which is to weaken the aggressor without adding aught to his cause. We have seen an over-eager amateur boxer draw back and summon his most powerful blow for his opponent only to fan the air in chagrin and disappointment.

The surest way to exhaustion and defeat is to rush to one's tasks in the morning with nerves so tense that the hand is unsteady. The desire to do an enormous amount of work blazes so hotly in our hearts that it burns up our energies in the process. Our disappointment at the failure only increases our disability, and the day wanes and closes with emptiness of results.

"But what of our attitude toward evil? Should not our indignation burn hotly against that?" Assuredly; and we ought not even to squint our eyes at wrong. More, there are many wrongs which, if we look them full in the face, will arouse the deepest antagonism of our nature. But indignation may burn like a blue-flame of the laboratory—quietly, softly, yet all the more intensely, and to a purpose, *viz.*, the fusing of elements in the crucible. This is far better than a spectacular conflagration that would destroy the whole laboratory, along with crucible and fused elements. Fiery enthusiasm is too often self-destructive, as well as being fatal to a good cause.

Evils can frequently be rectified by a non-resistive, even friendly attitude. Many a criminal, who is considered the incarnation of wickedness, might be brought to a better life by the application of this principle. Some good "Bishop of D——," leads a Jean Valjean to a life of honor and usefulness, not by testifying against him for stealing silver, but by shielding him, in very kindness, from the iron hand of the law

which has nothing humanitarian in it. Harshness never yet brought out the little good that
remained dormant in the felon's heart. Some time
we shall learn that our system of punishment is
grossly wrong, even from an economic standpoint, not to mention any higher basis. Some
day we will place in charge of the criminal class
our strongest, best, most skilled men, whose wisdom will make them kind, and whose knowledge
will enable them to recognize that a long fulcrum
is better than a short one if you would prize a
stranded ship out of the mud.

Yes, evil is to be overcome, overpowered, if
you please; but how? By non-resistance. "Re-
sist not evil." If I am insulted, the hot rejoinder
does not bring about an apology, but only renews
the quarrel. "Turning the other side" may
bring, not only an apology, but may cause the
pouring of oil into the wounds of the smitten
cheek on the part of the insulter. "The other
side," gives the enemy a chance to see from a
new viewpoint. The smitten side is covered with
blood—and blood ever whets the lion's appetite.
The bloodless side has no suggestion of conflict;
it is neutral, pacificatory in its appearance. If
everybody had been able to look at this other
side in 1860 we would have had no Civil War.

For "the other side" is ever the side of kindness, brotherliness.

We worry ourselves sick over insults, real or imagined wrongs. Men smite our cheek; then what? Turn the other side and let them smite that, too? That would seem to be the command of the great Teacher. But what of the ruffian, the villain, the coarse, ill-bred person? Let the same thug beat our faces black on one side and blue on the other? Permit the boor to tread upon our toes, and then extend the other foot for the same treatment? An answer to these questions demands more than categorical statements. Certainly, one must defend oneself against thieves and robbers; the perpetuation of the race requires that. But self-defense does not extend to the point of the aggressive punishment which the world is wont to give. It sometimes becomes necessary for a parent to hold the hands of his angered, raging child, but to brutally wound and hurt him would be wrong. The father has only been turning the other side— the side of kindness—by firmly gripping the youngster's arms until the storm of wrath is lulled. The child is thereby conquered by kindness, and readily capitulates to love. And that is the very kernel of the divine teaching—to rise above passion, and be able to display to the offender such a fraternal and sympathetic side of character that he will be attracted by it and strive to emulate it. "A soft answer turneth away wrath"; but what of a harsh reply? If half the world would begin to speak gently to angered, maddened souls, the other half would catch up the vibrations of sweetness just as one violin string responds to the vibrations of another string that has been plucked.

We too frequently manifest the resistive attitude in the performance of our tasks. We go at them as if we were in a sparring-match, battling against, instead of falling in with, the current of forces that we are to utilize. The way to master the current of a stream is to swim with it; then, the otherwise antagonist becomes our helper. Our real task in life is to direct, not overcome, forces. One overcomes evil in another individual, not so much by attacking the evil as by bringing out the good. To attack the evil only establishes a storm-center there, occupies the attention of the person attacked, and makes him neglectful of the good that may lie dormant within. To focalize his mind upon the good in himself brings into play the identical psychic laws, and the evil is thereby overlooked. Evil is ever overcome by substitution, not annihilation; by displacement rather than destruction.

The business man that goes to his desk in the resistive attitude is fighting against his best forces —those that are within. The back of his neck is rigid, his spinal column stiff, the nerves of his entire body tense. It requires much energy to sustain these attitudes—energy that ought to be expended upon the piles of papers that lie before him. And long before he is through them, the neck is tired, the small of the back is in a rack of pain, while the whole nervous system is in rebellion against unjust treatment. All through the day this man was fighting against his tasks, and the harder he stuck at them, the more fiercely they rebounded, just as a punching-bag flies back into a boy's face from the impact of harder blows. No wonder worries multiplied as the day waned until, well-nigh distracted, he closed his desk with a sigh and a groan. What the man needed to have made it different was a better understanding of the gospel of relaxation and non-resistance.

We fight our vexations scientifically not by resisting, but rather by letting them swing past us. Keep out of the path of worries and proceed with your work, is a good rule. If you try

to quit worrying you will fail; if you go heartily
to your task, you are obliged to forget worries.
"How do you get along with doubts?" asked a
parishioner of a minister. "I don't have time
to bother with them," was the reply. And there
is sound philosophy in the answer. There are
enough positives in life to keep us busy without
wasting our time on negatives. In learning to
ride a bicycle I found from experience what I
could not understand from theory, that the way
to break the spell of an object to be avoided is
to remove the eyes from it. We become object-
struck by our vexations. All day we run with
our disappointments as the most prominent objects of consideration; is it wonderful that we
come into them as the day closes, and find ourselves stunned by the sudden collision?

A seemingly different principle, yet virtually
the same as that which has so far been enun-
ciated, needs to be noticed; some enemies, instead of being avoided, need merely to be ap-
proached in a friendly way. It is safer to stand
squarely and face a fierce canine than to run
from him across an open field. If you fly, you
are sure to be caught and bitten. Your flight
only intensifies the fierceness and sense of superiority of the snarling animal. The part of wis-

dom is to "make up" to the enemy; speak kindly, gently, and without trace of fear. If once you can lay your hand on his head and give a friendly stroke, you are safe. If you meet a headache in the way, the part of wisdom may not be to run from it in dread, fear or hate, by the use of anesthetics; it is often better to "make up" to the headache by the use of mental medicine, which is nothing more than a friendly attitude. A fierce, raging ache or pain is likely to become docile under such treatment. Skill and strategy are as much needed in our daily struggles with ourselves as they are on the great fields of battle, where mighty armies face each other.

We need the friendly attitude toward a conscience which is ever bringing to us a sense of self-condemnation and disgust with the past. I am aware that we should despise wickedness and sinfulness, but we should not hate ourselves. When conscience comes to you and sneers, "Behold your historic self; see that piece of evil in your former life; do you think you should ever respect yourself again?" you need to hold up before conscience the better part of the past. Present to her deeds of goodness, and lay before her days upon days of clean, wholesome struggle after the truth. You will find conscience mollified, softened, gentler. And that attitude is not the self-righteous one; it is merely "turning the other side" of your soul's countenance, and saving yourself from a wholesale and destructive self-condemnation. If you keep nothing but your past life before conscience, she will burn your soul into a veritable crisp under the spur and goad of the enmity that is ever flaunted in her face. Turn the other side, saying to her: "Here, in the home circle, is the noble desire; there, in the school life, is the high ambition; and yonder, by the brook, under the old oak, is the deep yearning after God and Truth."

It is then that the fretting guardian of men's happiness will become calm and friendly, loving and kind; and with locked arms, you and your conscience may walk down the pathway together in the bonds of congenial fellowship. Both—you and your conscience—have won; the integrity of the right has been vindicated; you are on friendly terms with yourself and the whole world. And finally, you have prepared yourself in attitude for a friendly acquaintance with the universe as a whole, spreading as it does into the limitless spaces beyond the little ball on which we live and move.

Chapter IV

THE ABIDING PASSION

WE need pause here to fortify our minds against the absorption of a concept of life which, because of its speciousness, may lead us into a false position as to our relations with the elements of the material sphere to which our present existence is limited. We must be careful in our definition of friendliness to acquire a virile and vigorous attitude in our interpretation of the term. There is to be nothing anemic implied in the objective of friendliness, nor of calm complacency as we view the clash of forces on the battleground of the soul. Yea, more; there is a profound moral oughtness resting upon us that declares man's attitude should be *enthusiastically* friendly to the forces about him. It is necessary to view this earth as a field of human activity in which there is a tremendous amount of work to do. And each man, to be true to his destiny, is under moral necessity of having his hands overflowingly full of tasks that have been set by the Creator as the creature's part.

The most miserable class in the world, whether composed of surfeited rich, or helpless poor, is that aggregation of individuals who have nothing to do. Close up to this company of folk is the yet larger class which has plenty to do, but is unhappy in the doing of it. The Fates preserve us from being in either!

It is pleasing to see a man interested and happily absorbed in his work. His business may consist in mending shoes, but if he is thoroughly and contentedly entertained by his tasks, he is to be congratulated. There are few finer spectacles in the work-a-day world than that of this same cobbler, singing over his last, week upon week, until finally he comes down to a certain day which marks the end of his shoe-mending. Despite that pain in his side, he puts the finishing touch on the little patch, gives a final gloss to the heel and sole, shuts up shop for ay, and goes home in the consciousness that he has completed an honest job.

If we were to inquire closely into the philosophy of life as held by this humble man, we should likely get very little that would be illuminating. The best we should hear would probably be something like this: "I have striven to make an honest living for my wife and children, and in doing so, it was a pleasure to render satisfaction to my patrons." And I would not sneer at the philosophy of industry and common honesty in bread-winning; would that it might spread to all quarters and into all vocations!.

If we ascend the ladder from this lowest industrial rung, which touches the ground at the cobbler's shop, we may find at the top the manufacturer of shoes, who has taken much pride and expended great pains in building up the reputation of his output. Maybe he has enjoyed the commendable feat of succeeding, and it has been intoxicating to him to meet competition and overcome it. He has long since passed the mark of merely making a living for his family; it hardly enters into his head from day to day to count bread-winning as an object in life to him. It is the game of business, the luxury of success, the stimulant of winning out in the contest that brings him .joy. One day he ends his respectable career, and is eulogized as an example of thrift and good citizenship—and those are no mean encomiums, either. It ought to be gratifying, indeed, to any man to feel that, when he is gone, plaudits so honorable will be passed upon him.

Despite all the good we could say of both men, however, if we stop with the preceding ac-

counts of the lives of the cobbler or manufacturer, there is something unsatisfactory in the
contemplation. If the joy of the one consisted
in honest bread-winning, and that of the other in
business success, we must turn away from them
if we would find true exemplars. We feel the
want of types with more in them of what I shall
call soul-passion. There may be a sort of passion
for money-making in the heart of either, or both,
but it is not the abiding passion. One would just
as readily recommend the passion of shoe-mender
as shoemaker; neither rises above the earth, and
both die with the bodies of the two men.

I have taken a typical example in each case out
of the commercial world to make foundation for
the axiomatic statement above, that neither contains the very highest element of soul-passion,
which is a compound resultant of the finest forces
of intellection and emotion, emanating from the
fiery furnace of an inspired will.

We naturally turn to some masters in science
or art for an example of devotion to causes and
aims that entitles it to the high rank of soul-
passion. Well may we remove the sandals from
our feet lest we offend the spirits that hover
around the burning bush of science. For I honor
and revere the men who have literally given their

lives for the cause of knowledge, and not a few of whom have suffered a martyr's death. Beautiful to see the artist, all aglow with the passion for his ideal, and bowing his head in a last rest, with glazed eyes yet turned toward his beloved painting. Impressive and tragic to note the chemist in his laboratory surrendering his life in the discovery of a new but deadly poisonous gas. Wonderful, wonderful! Stand with reverent heart in the presence of Charles Darwin, whose whole life was spent in the ardent pursuit of truth. He worked continuously, and, according to the testimony of his son, worked very rapidly, begrudging every lost moment as being more precious than gold. And who, without deepest emotion, can behold Livingstone, in the heart of Africa, dying, with the last notes of his discoveries lying hard by, the words of which are fairly a-quiver with the life of his intense spirit?

And yet, if the passion of these apostles of knowledge went no further than the cold chronicles of their studies and discoveries, it must subside and pass as being unable to burn with the luster of unfading suns. The really abiding passion is that which lives beyond any particular cycle of time, and which actually projects itself into an eternal world.

Measure by this standard of the abiding passion, my cobbler; his honest, industrious life, with all of its attractiveness, is an evanescent thing, unless you might link it with a great passion, such as moved William Carey. He was just such a shoemaker as I have described, plus the real difference that lifts a man out of mediocrity into immortality; for while he tacked soles and sewed up rents in old leather, there flashed down into his heart a flame from the eternal altars which led him to turn his eyes toward far-off India, where the god of Lust ruled with relentless power a quarter billion slaves. As this flame burned in Carey's heart he plied himself to the study of the nations and their languages, and, following its ever-brightening light, went as a rescuer of the hopeless. His passion for their deliverance led him to fight for years for the abolishment of the inhuman suttee, and the glory of its passing belongs to the shoemaker. "Shoemaker, stick to your last," as a motto for the good repairing of old shoes is very well; but it can never manacle a life like that of the great missionary, whose chief glory was that he linked India with the universe by the cords of eternal happiness.

Leap many steps higher on the ladder of time

and consider Darwin. It is thoroughly altruistic of him, as he writes to a friend, to lament that, twenty million years hence, the earth will be frozen down to its fiery heart, and myriads of men, good, noble-souled humans, will have perished off the face of the earth for lack of food and warmth. Passion truly burns in his heart for his race, but I am persuaded that it falls short of the abiding sort, for a man with the abiding type can never give up, never let go the human family. He can not, with the blue-flame of his love for the race flashing through his brain, conceive of death and cold annihilation.

And that other scientific man, Livingstone: He explored Africa, discovered lakes and rivers, opened up the dark continent to the world, and it is eminently just that, as a mere explorer, his remains should rest in Westminster Abbey. But the abiding passion was what carried Livingstone to Africa's heart; the passion for the freedom of men, the breaking of slave-shackles. This passion kept him up, sustained him to the very last day, and Livingstone, dead upon his knees in prayer, in the lonely wilderness, but representing an undying cause, is mightier than a living man, linked to the carcass of temporal selfishness.

It seems very clear, if the above statements are

in line with truth, that there can be no abiding passion apart from a profound racial love. There is no such thing as a great and intense passion for rocks, rivers, oceans, flowers, except as those things borrow human interest from the beings that quarry the rocks, explore the rivers, navigate the oceans, and inhale the fragrance of the flowers. Talk of Hugh Miller's passion for rocks; only go deep enough, drill through granite and sandstone strata, and finally you will strike into the folds and recesses of the human heart. And we think of Wordsworth as loving the flowers with a deep, personal feeling; ay, that is exactly what it is after all, for do we hear him saying,

"To me the meanest flower that blows can give
Thoughts that do often lie too deep for tears?"

And where, pray, are the depths whose emotions can not at all be translated in the terms of tears? Verily, in the human soul. I like that saying of Saint Paul's: " . . . the Spirit himself maketh intercession for us with groanings that can not be uttered." Beneath all our tongues and languages, our fine talk and oratory, our heartrending words along with mystic hints of the poet, there is a deep, inexpressible sob in the whole universe for the uplift of Man!

It requires a wonderful passion to sustain itself to life's end. Physical desire, sometimes called passion, is far from so doing. Yonder old, withered man looks in surprize, sometimes even with contempt and impatience, on the hot-blooded-ness of unrestrained youth. He has almost forgotten. Even family ties become brittle, like oxidized, rotten iron rods, which once held great structures together. The wrinkled brow is scarcely lifted at news of death of some far-off relative or friend. It is too late to mourn, then; there are, in truth, no tear-springs from which to draw; long since they were dipt dry, down to the dregs which are only as ashes now.

But just one object does keep him in touch with deep, subterranean springs; it is the redemption scheme of the race, whereby men are freed from the overwhelming weight of sin. That same old man, apart from the crowd, out of touch with the passing world, has an abiding interest in the disenthrallment of men's hearts. "He is in the sere leaf, is childish, now; takes no notice of the affairs of life," the young and thoughtless are saying. They think him a dotard; in reality, they themselves are fools, since the very things that they consider worth while are merest rubbish, while the real treasures of life are to them useless burdens that retard progress to the land of mirth.

And herein lies the most powerful dynamic that ever thrilled and kept fresh to its purpose a human heart. In the fact of redemption as promulgated in the Christian scheme there is an undying and continuously rejuvenating force that causes us to marvel without ceasing as we experience its application. The passion of a Christian can never die, inasmuch as it emanates from those eternal sources of the universe that have their origin in the heart of God. And so, it becomes perfectly logical to the reflecting mind that religious enthusiasm should glow with supernal brightness, even amid the ashes of dying physical embers.

And I can not refrain here from declaring that one of the chief sustaining elements of the soul's abiding passion, emanating from the redemptive life of Jesus, is the constructive character of the work which such passion contemplates. I conceive that no work is so high and satisfying as the creative act, and it is the glory of that sensation which is imparted to the human spirit as it grapples with other spirits and helps them past the throes of the new birth into the Kingdom of God. The mind so engaged is aglow with the zest, the ecstacy, the supreme joy of the universe. Surely, God could grant to the sons of men no loftier privilege than that of helping Him in the creation of a new empire, furnished with inhabitants who were created anew, cast in the mold of the Son of Man. If one could reconstruct, by divine help, the picture of a God turning new planets from His hand, and could see the triumphant glory of His face, it would then be possible to know the joy of a human soul, in the white heat of passionate love, lifting the dying soul of a brother into the realm of life.

The abiding passion has one of its chief supports in a sustained interest, which ever undergirds it. The soul never becomes weary in its zealous quest, never afraid or ashamed. Surfeit and *ennui,* those death-dealing cankers to myriads of lives, can get no hold on the heart.

It is a fatal thing to lose interest in one's outlook, to cease to have a keen concern for the development of one's resources, the exalting of one's calling, the full accomplishment of one's task. Nobody can be absolutely safe from the attacks of satiety and disgust that prey upon so many mortals, except as the soul is aglow with

the abiding passion for the timeless welfare of
men.

One of the marvelous things about this master-
passion is that it demands, inherently, by its very
nature, conflict and struggle in order to perpetuate
itself. There was never a saint that went through
the world without struggle and hardship. This
conflict feeds the flame that burns for the world,
and sets an example to others that is ever a
source of inspiration and encouragement. The
fiercest warfare is that which is waged on a
spiritual basis; the severest of all battles is that
which rages upon the plains of a soul aflame with
divine passion.

The impassioned soul is, by its universal sympathy for men, the truly cosmopolitan spirit of
the globe. No commercial or scientific aims can
lead a man into a deep and cooperative sympathy
with all races and tribes. The castes of India
will not yield to material forces alone; only the
battering-rams of a spiritual host can complete
the destruction of such adamantine walls. But
the impassioned soul, illumined by eternal fires,
is restrained by no boundary lines in the realm of
creation, and the sphere of her sovereignty shall
extend as far as discovery goes.

Chapter V

BONDAGE AND FREEDOM

DESPITE the glory of the abiding passion as a heaven-born gift, I often reflect with solicitude upon the dangers that threaten its possessors. Religion offers the richest of all fields for the nurture of wisdom, but it is sadly true that folly springs like a mushroom out of the same rich soil unless constant guard is exercised against it. The religionist who has lost his bearings is of all men most to be pitied. And the course between a fanatical abandon to divine guidance, apart from profound reflection, and a conceited self-consciousness that deems outside influence needless, is indeed difficult to pursue under certain circumstances. And yet it is a possibility; and the possibility lies in the conscious sovereignty of the mind, which, while recognizing the supreme rulership of the Sovereign of the universe, nevertheless looks upon that sovereignty delegated to the individual as being a most sacred trust. No man has a right to cease thinking for himself. God not only permits but demands of the individual intellectual independence. He that permits others to think for him is no longer free, and so, in its high and true sense, is no longer a *man*.

The anthropoid ape, with a brain strikingly like man's, lives in the woods, feeds upon the wild fruits that grow there, climbs tree-trunks, leaps in frolicsome mood from limb to limb, or with evident delight swings pendant from favorite boughs by hands marvelously like our own. But the ape dies, leaving the forest just the same, while the course of brook and river remains unchanged. If he had only possest reason, the ape could have lived in a mansion and turned the wilderness into a city. Just because man thinks, he cuts down trees which the ape left intact, lives in a house instead of the naked forest, builds cities where jungles grew, makes deserts blossom, drains swamps, turns the course of rivers, navigates oceans, and makes the very air a medium of transportation. To trace what thought has done is to go the whole course of civilization to the present; to prophesy what it will yet do is to lay oneself liable to the charge of being a fantastic dreamer or an apostle of wild vagaries.

And yet, with all that thought has done, it is far more important that we ourselves should know how to think rather than know the substance of what others have thought. To be able to think for oneself is far better than to follow the beaten path of other minds; a nugget of truth which one has digged by one's own effort out of the mine of knowledge is of more value to its possessor than a whole heap of truths that one finds assorted by the wayside. Knowing how to think is equivalent to being independent in one's thought.

But it needs to be stated at the outset that by independence in thinking I do not mean absolutely and unrelated original thought, for I very seriously question whether any man has ever achieved such an end, or could achieve it by his mightiest effort. Who knows if he ever had an original thought? He who credits himself with such a feat is likely to find this seeming discovery in some volume as old as Aristotle—that is, if one means by original thought that which no one else ever had. But if one means by the term, original thought, the quality of originality so far as it concerns the thinker himself, and his methods of work, the application may be quite befitting. A vigorous, active mind may acquire much knowledge in a truly independent manner, if we take fearlessness and self-confidence within the bounds of our definition, and the benefits to such a mind are of inestimable value.

A fearless, self-confident attitude, therefore, lies at the base of all independent thinking. Not every man who can fearlessly execute the thoughts of others can, with equal boldness, assert his own, or even freely think his own thoughts. Some there are who would put on the armor of Saul and go forth with boldness, who would not dare meet the giant with a sling of their own making, nor feel well armed with a few stones gathered from the brook by themselves. We are literally afraid to think in many of the important spheres of conduct.

One field of thought where men tread lightly and are afraid is that of politics. Comparatively few voters are independent in the matter of suffrage. They may go to the polls with much zest and loud hurrahing, but some one else has made out the ticket and prepared the campaign thunder. It requires an amount of courage that the majority do not possess to prepare one's own ballot and do one's own thundering.

Equally true it is that most of the world is afraid to think in that widest of all realms, religion. We are what we are, religiously, because we happen to be born heirs to certain tenets and beliefs. Sometimes we look longingly at the realm of freedom, but are prevented entering it through fear.

Not a few, likewise, are possest of certain elements of moral cowardice. They see things that disgust and sicken them, but they are afraid to break the images of their classes. Many a woman looks with longing eye to the companionship of a true, lofty soul in a different circle, but is hindered in her desire to go to her through fear alone.

Even more lamentable still, perhaps, than many of the existing forms of bondage is the fact that most students in our schools and colleges do not acquire that independence in their methods of thought that entitles them to a place in the principality of freedom. The student is really serving an apprenticeship while mastering the curriculum of his school, and if, like Wilhelm Meister, he can be granted the diploma of a free man when once the course is finished, he is to be warmly praised. Happy the man who, coming out from the cloister of learning, to knock for admission into the circle of world-toilers, can say, "I come as an independent thinker and actor."

One of the depressing things the teacher has to contemplate in the character of his students is a species of fetish-worship which ties them down to the letter of the law in the books. Not that I would discount the book as a criterion of accuracy, for knowledge, to be knowledge at all, must first be accurate. But the accuracy of an automaton is far less to be admired than the accuracy of a free mind, untrammeled by bias and irksome rule. It is a lack of courage that makes the student in algebra turn nervously ever and anon to the back of his book to get the assurance of the answer to be found there. He shows clearly that he is afraid to trust his own work. The girl who eagerly seeks her companion to know how she construes a lesson in Virgil is yet too timid for the hard tasks of life where she will be thrown upon her own resources, there to triumph through courage and strength of self-confidence, or to fail through the cowardice and weakness of self-distrust.

Our object in subjecting ourselves to the study of books and the mastery of curricula of certain institutions of learning is to become free, intellectually, not enslaved. If one comes out from this tutelage the possessor of many facts of history and science, and yet afraid to think independently, one has become a slave, not a free man or woman. The highest freedom that is known or that can be imagined is intellectual freedom. There came a time in history when the Romans became masters to the Greeks, but the Greek slave, tho bodily in duress, became master to his master because he was his master's teacher.

There is a bondage to books that is servile. The right use of books is of prime importance to the student. He should love them as his friends and companions, use them as his faithful servants and tools, but serve them as his masters, never. Take your book-slave, and consider his state of body and mind. If he would have a drink of water, he must run to the book to inquire what the analysis is, and what the books say. If the books say, do not drink, he allows his lips to parch and his tongue to crack with thirst. If he would evolve a philosophy of life, he must turn to a certain page to see what a favorite work on sociology would declare; or, if he would have an ultimatum on capital and labor, "To the book! to the book!" he cries, and it is settled as he dogmatically and smilingly points his finger to what the Absolute says. To him there is no interpretation of a Scripture without a commentary and the standards of theology. The book-slave never gets beyond the country in which he was born, and even that land is not possest in his own name;

for he exists there only by permission of certain feudal lords who hold him in vassalage. He has a mortal terror of treading the unknown lands of thought unaccompanied by his liege lord. His creed shuts out from consciousness the fact that the grandest heroes of the world have been those that have prest into the forests, and across the deserts of life, alone, and, after rough voyages, have planted the standard of truth in countries beyond some unknown sea.

I would not be understood as looking with scorn upon books, for I place the highest value upon them. They are the student's best friends and his most useful servants, and they do more for him than all other friends or servants so long as they are used of him in these capacities. I can think of no picture more highly ideal than that of an independent student, in his library, looking affectionately—shall I not say it?—upon the loved volumes on the shelves. Ruskin likens books to princes and queens, mutely gazing upon their owners, and proffering their companionship.

I rejoice to say that some of my warmest friends are among the books with which I associate daily. I have but to run the eye along yonder shelf, and I see two friends among the poets—Wordsworth and Tennyson. And there come days when I simply must have converse with them. How many times, when pent up in the confines of the city, with nerves a-tingle from its clang of noises, have I sought and found the peace of the country in Wordsworth's "Lines," written near Tintern Abbey! Or, some sonnet, some tender little tribute to lowly celandine or daisy has brought me the needed rest and solace. And my heart has found encouragement, as I have opened that volume of Tennyson, and turned to the worn leaves where I read with a feeling of uplift the deep soul-utterances of "Locksley Hall." For that poem, mark you, is no mere sentiment, or puling wail of a love-sick youth, but rather the struggle of a broken spirit to gain its footing again in the world of heroic service. Often, too, has my heart been steadied in times of doubt as I have followed another's struggles and triumphs in "The Two Voices," or, as in that longer poem, "In Memoriam," I have battled against the mystery of sorrow into a reconciliation to the divine will.

And what lover of books does not have his favorite master in fiction, to whom he goes anon for refreshment as he feels the burdens of life grow heavy? And there, too, is some old classic, perhaps from Greek or Roman, which is golden to us, and works like magic in bringing one into the normal attitude of mind and heart. Times there are when the soul literally yearns for companionship and help which there is no human hand to offer. To such a being, books, messages from the world's greatest dead, become one of the priceless boons of existence, bringing the fellowship of redemption from despair.

Independence in thinking, like the independence of a country, does not mean the isolating of oneself from another's influence, but the wise mastery of one's own mind to such an extent that it can best obtain help from other minds. The original thirteen colonies of America fought hard for independence, and won it by great sacrifice of life and blood. But that does not mean that the United States to-day receives no benefits from England; indeed, our country could scarcely conceive of a commercial, literary or religious existence apart from the direct influence of the mother country. We hold the citadels of power, certainly; our guns bristle from every fort, as men-of-war fly our flag on all seas and under all suns for the defense of that precious thing we call liberty. But what would become of us if vessels of peace, laden with commerce and goodwill, ceased to pass betwixt us and England? As

our country is independent of England, and yet
dependent upon her in so many ways, so one's
mind may be independent of the tyranny of books,
but wisely dependent upon them for needed supplies and influence.

As a youth I knew a hard old schoolmaster.
When he wished to vent his wrath upon a boy
against whom he had no just grievance, he bade
the object of his ill-will, upon a certain occasion,
"look at the sun until he saw stars." Going to
the door the lad looked, with blinking eyes, and,
half-blinded and dizzy, returned crestfallen to the
master. "I saw no stars," said he. "Then look
again," commanded the master. The lad looked,
and again with tear-filled eyes, declared most hon-
estly that he saw none. "Well, look till you do
see stars!" stormed the master of the ferule.
Whereupon, the ingenious youth, taking recourse
to falsehood, upon glancing up at the sun the
third time profest quite glibly, "Yes, sir, I see
stars." "Aha! aha!" chuckled the master
fiendishly, "You have now told me a falsehood.
Hold out your knuckles, you wretch, and I will
make them tingle!"

I am glad to believe that schoolmasters of
that type are very rare, and that such harshness
belongs to a day that is gone. But I am sure

that it is quite possible, even in this golden time, to be the base servant of books to such an extent that when the books command the reader to see stars, he will, blinking and squinting and rubbing his eyes say, nevertheless, "Oh, yes, I see stars and they are so beautiful!" Such an unintelligent and insincere acquiescence is falsehood of the most subtle sort, for it cheats the deluded confessor out of that richest of all possessions, mental integrity.

Dr. Corson has somewhere compared the brain of a certain type of educated man to a well-kept hayloft. In that storehouse of the farmer there are bundles of oats and fodder, bales of hay and other provender, which the owner can get on demand. If he wants oats for his horse, he knows where to get them; in the dark, likewise, he can lay hand upon a bundle of fodder, since everything is in its place. In like manner, the mechanically educated man under consideration has a well-stored mind; Greek roots and Latin verbs and mathematical formulae are all carefully placed in their respective corners. If you ask the owner of this brain-loft to construe a Greek or Latin sentence, he has but to reach up to the proper compartment for the rules of grammar and syntax, and the work is done. If you call for the solution of a problem in mathematics he can reach into the "loft" and find a formula by which he can perform the task. But ask him to preach a sermon on the text, "I am come that ye might have life," and he will tell you that he never learned how, and therefore, can not do it.

Such a person, tho trained to acquire facts, is only a slave to his acquirements, and knows not the freedom of a liberated mind. In striking contrast to such a human machine is that individual who acquires facts of knowledge unceasingly, but who takes the formal truth so obtained down into the laboratories of God, and there welds them, over the blue-flame of divine love, into a glowing compound with the Spirit of the universe. The resultant is a mind charged with intelligent enthusiasm; a soul filled with the dynamics of the storm and yet capable of orderly movement, expending all its forces for constructive development, wasting none in useless devastation.

The age is in need of a religion that has reason at its base, a spirituality that combines rational principles with supra-rational elements, thus making a compound that commends itself to God and man. That type of religion which represents a state of fervid ebullition, and uses spirituality as a safety-valve for surplus steam-power is not desirable. Of that we have had quite enough. It may be well for the race to work off its surplus energy through football and other vigorous forms of athletics, to allow large freedom to the imagination in relieving the mind of the sensation of over-fulness; but to turn our religion into an exhibition of spiritual gymnastics is totally abhorrent to any well-poised, reflecting mind.

Chapter VI

AS A MAN THINKETH

THE important objective of individuality as exemplified in intellectual independence is basic to the attainment of a new selfhood, much as the first rung of a ladder is essential as a medium of reaching a second rung. The whole universe is so related that no one planet or star could exist alone, altho each orb possesses a noble individuality that is separate and distinct from that of all others. And as this entire universe represents an expanded whole as an essential unity, preserving at the same time the integrity of component parts, so does the infinite Mind of the Spiritual universe represent an indestructible unity, within which the myriads of human minds find their individuality. The objective of each of these individual minds is to discover its proper relation to the infinite Spirit. Until that balance and relation is found, the mind of a man is much like a planet would be if it should veer from its orbit and thus lose equilibrium with its sun. Destruction would of necessity ensue.

The finite runs the risk of losing its supreme opportunity through a terrible clash with the Infinite. Granted a proper equilibrium with the Infinite, and the finite mind has the privilege of a destiny in every way glorious.

Viewed in this light, we may consistently think of man as being in a certain sense the perfection of his own creation. Not only is he a co-worker with God in bringing about a new creation as pertains to others, but he is God's first lieutenant in the re-creation of himself. He is moving along the orbit of thought toward a central Mind, from which all thought emanates. As man approaches this Mind, his experience is analagous to that of a metal which advances through increasing stages of temperature toward the fusing point. For the soul of man reaches a white heat of intensity as it touches the mind of God, and at last reaches a fusing point; man dwells in God, and God in man. For only by thinking the thoughts of the Creator can humanity become like Him.

But looking about me, I must take an inventory of my resources as well as responsibilities. If I am to reach my new destiny along the path of thought, is it necessary for me to consider any other factor in destiny than that of spirit or pure thought? That might all depend upon the fact of the existence of something other than mind. Is there aught else? Am I to strive after an idealism that eliminates matter as a negligible quantity in the higher reaches of the spirit? But if matter is only an appearance, it does not necessarily follow that I am to neglect it in my calculations; if it is a reality, then it must become some sort of a factor in the processes by which I am to reach my true relation to Him who made both matter and spirit. It may be that, granting the non-reality of matter, its apparent existence is a workable essential with which to reach God; that without the appearance as a blind, the soul would be overcome with the dazzling brightness of the great Reality.

I would briefly, then, sum up a simple philosophy of mind and matter: Certain mental scientists are fond of saying there is nothing in the world except mind. Most of us, however, are dualists, and think of life as embracing two entities, one material and the other spiritual. I confess to being in this latter class. For while to my mind the material part of the world is but a shell for the spirit, I am bound to accord the shell an essential place under the present conditions of existence. No one ever saw a rose's beauty ex-

cept in the rose's petals; likewise, the only beautiful soul any one ever knew was living in "a
house of clay." Angels are no doubt beautiful
to those that can see them, but no one can see a
spirit until one enters a spiritual world.

And yet, for all that, we are agreed that the
moral side of life is entirely inherent in the
spiritual part. A stone or tree can not sin, neither
can the hand or tongue or foot of a human being.
The attitude of mind is the determining factor as
to the rightness or wrongness of an act. If the
mind's attitude is bad, the body, like an automaton, does bad things; the fingers filch, the
tongue swears, the eye beholds and the ear hears
the foul. But if the mind be honest, the fingers
will never take what belongs to another; if it be
truly reverent, the tongue will not be profane; if
truly good, the eye will see through the shell of
badness to the inner goodness, while the ears will
translate the tuneless jargon of the world into
veritable heavenly music. The mind carries the
body around with it as a servant, and "the servant is not greater than his lord."

Is a man responsible for what he thinks? Do
men and God hold him accountable? Most assuredly. Then, what is it that thinks? It is the
mind, the ego. The brain is only a medium for

thought. The personal self is responsible at the bar of the eternal Truth for the way it uses this medium. The account must be rendered with the utmost precision, for when the mind thinks a certain thing, the brain registers it, and that single registration is an influencing factor in causing the mind to entertain the same thought again. The two—brain and mind—become reciprocal in their influence. A mind that is bad can not become good until cell-changes have taken place in the brain. For that reason, a bad, old man is very difficult to render good, and a good man, who has advanced to maturity, stands like a Gibraltar against onslaughts of evil. The bending of the young tree until it has become fixt in its shape is a favorite figure, used as an analogy between the tender plant and tender youth. If a boy can only get through his teens clean-minded, and free from bad habits, we feel that he is safe—and he generally is. It is simply the result of law, inexorably fixt but wondrously kind.

What a man thinks determines, therefore, what he is. He *is* what he thinks, for there is really no more to him. He has a material body and brain, but these are totally subservient to what he thinks. The brain can change only as it is directed to change, and when it has reached a certain age it is very slow to unlearn the lessons of youth. The reflex centers have become so well established after a certain age that they refuse to be over-thrown.

Thought acts like a boomerang—it always comes back just as it went out, no better, no worse. If it is kind and clean, it comes back so; if hateful and impure, it returns to the sender to make him more bitter and filthy. "Let him that is filthy be filthy still." We need to take earnest heed to our everyday thoughts, for in the progress of thinking we are only manufacturing ourselves over again, according to either a better or worse pattern than we formerly had. The brain refuses to stultify itself; it will be true to its teaching, even tho the teaching be bad. Continued lessons in debauchery are handed back to the master, Mind, which at last reaches a point where it is mastered by its own servant—a thing not unheard-of in many phases of existence. Every man is, to a large extent, the arbiter of his own destiny, especially in so far as that destiny relates to essential elements of character. There are vastly different brains to start with; some are coarse, some fine; some shaped for murder, others for kindness and love. But if taken under the right kind of tutelage soon enough, the regnant mind can turn the brain of a malefactor into that of a benefactor of the race, and the brain of a rogue into that of "an honest man, the noblest work of God." For this brain is the workshop, the mind is the smith, and thought is the product, whether it be delicate watch-spring, or the crude butcher-knife. The tendency, however, is to specialize, and if allowed to ply their butcher-knife business too long, both smith and shop will eventually become unfitted for the manufacture of watch-springs.

If men are held accountable for what they think, the evidence is *prima facie* that they can determine what they think in some considerable sense, else the law of responsibility would be inherently wrong. One is often heard to lament, "I can not govern my thoughts; they simply come and possess me, whether I will or no." But this statement is not true. It takes the hardest effort ever put forth by the will to govern the thoughts, but the task may be accomplished masterfully. It can be done, however, only under certain circumstances, and it is necessary to see to it that these circumstances are existent. Law is regnant there as everywhere else. No man can have wholesome thoughts if he choose surroundings that continually suggest the bad. We are all kindergarten pupils and shall ever use simple objects as means of knowledge. We can not frequent places where evil is supreme and expect to remain intact. If we make companions of books and people that are lacking in nobility of character, we thereby renounce the hope of rising to knighthood. But if we select such companionships in nature, and among books and people as will logically be suggestive of right and sound thinking, the mind, by law, follows the easier path. Will is a mighty being, but she needs every good angel to brace her up in her heavenly aspirations.

"As a man thinketh in his heart, so is he," does not suggest chance-thought; it indicates a clearly marked course and purpose. True, men may allow chance-circumstances to determine their thought, and so, the quality of life, but this is not a course that we must necessarily copy. If I am ever to have a high quality of character, I must deliberately choose to have it, and follow up the choice with a systematic effort, lasting through my whole life, toward the acquirement of goodness. If a man is "as he thinketh," the conclusion is inevitable that if he should cease to think, he would cease to be. Of course, it is impossible to cease entirely to think, yet it is quite easy to stop thinking vigorously. We not infrequently see a good man seemingly deteriorate in character, especially toward life's close. The cause? He first of all deteriorates in virility of thought. I have seen bright college men after getting into the routine of life, drop out of studious habits, and glide down to the lower levels of thought with the totally uneducated. The gold of character is molded at the mint of thought, but even gold will wear eventually, and if the mill ceases to turn as of yore, the current coin becomes scarce. The only method of keeping up a large circulation lies in coining more.

A man's real wealth inheres in what he thinks and how much he thinks. The mind must be occupied in some sort of fashion, and if it be not assigned the great and noble task it will take up the light and trivial one automatically. If the owner does not drive her maid-servant to hard work she will frisk and frolic on the green of mere pleasure, or wander into back alleys, there to revel in sluice-ponds of vice. The quality of one's thought may be rich, altogether good, or it may be poor, coarse and inferior. There is a deal of thought in the world comparable to certain fields —not vicious or bad, but simply barren and poor. This sort of thought needs what the poor land needs—some new ingredients. I believe that most of the poverty in the quality of thought arises from lack of interest, and from indifference. If men only concentrated, put intensity into their thought-fields, there would result a more luxuriant growth of products. Like skim-milk, all of the real richness of original thought has gone out by reason of standing. Constant shaking up is needed; a stirring of the vessel to its heart.

Strange to say, many men have had a few rich thoughts, and then dropt into seemingly hopeless poverty. They have made the impression that all reserve was used up, or that nothing but an inferior quality remained. That is one of the sad things in human experience: a sense of exhaustion—which all have felt, in some degree. Some one has said that Coleridge gave to the world only one complete work—"The Rime of the Ancient Mariner"—out of all that he began, but this one poem was indeed pure gold. But we all have a feeling of regret at wasted genius, believing that whoever could give to the race a treasure so rich as that matchless poem, might have digged up more from the hidden veins of the soul. A patch of ground in the mind rich enough to bring forth one luxuriant harvest will yield others if it be watered and tended. The valley of the Nile never has become poor, because of continuous yearly accretions by inundation. Every rich valley of the mind can experience a like fertilization if the owner will only open the flood-gates between himself and the infinite world, whose vast reservoirs are at the disposal of all of God's men.

The average mind may acquire great wealth by working zealously. A dozen or two of books, persistent application, joyous effort, brings the sure resultant—riches. There is no excuse for poverty of mind. Even the person too poor to have many books still has the *sine qua non* of all wealth—a brain, and a spirit behind it. If he but use what he has he is sure to possess more and more of the true riches. There is only one sort of poverty that is absolutely without excuse—that of soul-poverty. There are conditions beyond which I can not mount to procure material goods, but no obstacle is insurmountable between me and mental treasures. If I live and die a pauper it is my own fault, since no mortal can form a trust on good thinking nor create a combine by which a monopoly of mental products is acquired. Each soul is a sovereign whose realm reaches as far as industry and desire will extend it.

Of all riches in life the greatest is one's own self. It keeps us wondering, trying to understand. The soul rises like a sphinx, inscrutable, mysterious, on the plains of consciousness. Seen from one angle she seems to be one thing, from another point of view something vastly different. To-day she presents herself as an archangel of noblest purposes, while to-morrow she dons the garb of some evil genius. And yet, if I might call the soul a temple, and if every thought that passes through the brain were an entity, a part of the temple's furnishings, I could walk through the corridors and halls of the great structure and tell just what I am, for, "as a man thinketh in his heart, so is he." I should find every splendid rafter or rotten beam, each perfect painting or every miserable daub to be identically what I had placed there as master of the house. And seeing all of the good and bad, if I were wise, I should resolve never again to put in the house any painting except the finest, with the light of heaven shining upon it, nor ever to place aught of wooden work in the whole structure save that wrought out in Lebanon's mountains where finest cedars grow.

Chapter VII

THE NASCENT THOUGHT

IN the preceding pages I have discust mental activity more from its standpoint of quality than from that of method. It is necessary, therefore, to look into this latter principle, and inquire as to the best means of utilizing the product of thought. If the output of the mind were analogous to the output of a factory, and capable of being stored away like a stock of shoes or hats we might build up great fortunes in mind-stuffs and have a wonderful deal of wealth in ideas laid by on cold storage for future use. We could be just as unmethodical as we chose in thinking, and could lay by half-wrought concepts for future development. It would be as easy to carry thoughts around as it is for the market-women to carry her eggs to the trading mart in a basket. The most indolent man on earth could, on occasion, flash thoughts as precious as diamonds, having, perchance, gathered up a handful when the germs of laziness were inactive. But certain laws prevent such prodigal or improvident use of talent, and to these we may well turn our attention.

The atom, when first released from the grasp of its fellow, is called nascent. Being new-born, it really begins a new life. And the chemist tells us that only when this atom is young in its freedom is it strong and active. If it can possibly lay hold on some other free atom of the right kind, it will form a combination and help build a new molecule. The sooner it gets in touch with this other friendly atom the more stable is the combination, but the longer it remains uncombined the weaker is its hold upon the new companion. In even an atom's life the factor of time performs an important part.

Turning from the scientific to the psychic realm, we find there the analogous law that the nascent thought is the strongest, the most able to form combinations and accomplish work. The new thought, while the heat of enthusiasm is glowing in the brain, readily and eagerly does its tasks, but if the thought becomes old, it seems to lose its power. Thoughts, like men, become debilitated from want of activity. Men who do great things in life follow up their nascent thoughts, and grapple with a ready hand problems that only the new thought can solve. Men that do little in the world are those that nurse their thoughts and keep them stored up like bottled gases until they are old and stale, and have lost their pristine force. Like Hamlet, these men are dreamers, who may have purposes clear-cut enough, but do not carry them into execution.

One of the deep joys of life is that of evolving new thoughts. Other men may have had similar thoughts, but to the individual that generates them belongs true paternity. They are his own children, and as such are precious to him. That is, to the normal, rightly adjusted man. Only a monstrosity neglects his offspring and allows them to become old and dwarfed in the realms of their birth, without doing aught to push the world forward. The joy of thinking is supreme when these thoughts are put to work, and like mighty toilers are made to become producers. To see one's thoughts materializing into great factories, stores, machines or grain-fields kindles a divine fire of delight in one's eyes.

A great moral responsibility inheres in thinking. A man has no more right to allow his thoughts to die without accomplishing their work than a parent has to permit his children to grow up in idleness and bear no world-burdens. Since thinking differentiates human from brute, the power of thought is the Creator's pledge of favoritism to man. And he who does not highly prize his lofty position is grossly ungrateful; more, he is guilty of insult to the Author of his being.

Some souls that have worried a great deal and thought a little, fancy that thinking produces weariness, and consequently is to be indulged in parsimoniously. But it is worry, not thought, that produces the insupportable weariness of life. Thinking is only the natural outlet of pent-up mental energies, and is good for the normal man. The proper exercise of every function of our being is not only harmless; it is beneficial. If, as has been stated before, there are two billion cells in the human brain, not even the most active thinker can hope to use all of them in their every possible combination. At best, the brain may be said to have much territory that has not been utilized at the end of even a long career of toil. No man, in view of this fact, can justly fear that he will overdo his thinking powers, or overdraw his thought resources. A reservoir of perennial, ceaseless joy is at the command of every normal human being. All he has to do is to tap the fountain and let it run.

In what has been indicated above we have a triple key, a veritable open-sesame for all doors of achievement by men. That is, through mental activity work is done, happiness realized, and moral responsibility discharged. These three phases of life cover the whole gamut of human experience.

The power of unfoldment lies in the nascent thought. It drops sweetness as the maple sheds juices when first tapped; gives out aroma like the freshly crusht rose; sends forth refreshing waters like the mountain spring, which is purest and clearest at its source. But the old incision in the tree gives no tribute, the long-crusht rose is putrid, and the fountain's waters are corrupted far from the parent rock. To elaborate on the unfoldment, the more our fresh, new thoughts are utilized, the more do we have, as fresh and new as their forerunners were. Nothing save a new thought can beget a new thought. The man who uses his old sermon or lecture too long, finally wears it out by losing interest in it himself. Is it wonderful that those who hear him turn the smooth, well-worn phrases grow weary, too? The only way for the speaker to escape the *ennui* which he suffers is to get up a new speech. Then, as his own blood tingles with fresh life and joy, the pulse of his hearers also beats faster.

Some men seem wondrously stingy with their thoughts. So precious do they appear that they are put on the shelf to rot and waste. The finder of a new thought may lay it away in a napkin for safe keeping, only thereby to lose it. Let no man fear to use his thoughts, his very newest and best, for he will have more and better thoughts the next day. More: each one as it arrives will come like the bee from his morning rounds among new-blown flowers—laden with fresh sweets.

The more a man thinks, the more he does, for nothing performs work but thought. The bands and wheels and pulleys of a machine do not, in the absolute sense, work; it is the thought of the man who put them together. The engine, puffing and groaning before forty freight cars is not doing work—thought pulls the load. The horse drawing the plow is not the real worker; for the man at the handles furnishes the thought-energy which is the *sine qua non* of all accomplishment. The man who is not a thought-producer can never be called a world-worker of high grade. *Vice versa,* the man who thinks, in the true sense, is a worker whether his body moves or not. And to any one who thinks long enough and deeply enough all tasks eventually yield. It is impossible to think seriously without some measure of achievement.

No man who thinks in a normal way, ever evolving fresh thoughts, can have a gloomy time in life. Only as he begins to think again the old thoughts, to nurse them over-fondly, does he lose the zest and enjoyment that justly may be his. New thoughts, like new red blood, bring a glow to the cheek and health to the countenance. May the Fates deliver us from the brooding man, revolving in a diseased mind the imaginations or fancies of wrongs sustained in the past, until his whole soul is poisoned as the system is vitiated by re-breathing the same air.

The law of reproduction in the realm of thought gives rise to an ever-enlarging world of happiness. The infinite field of mind becomes an infinite field of enjoyment. Always there are new mountains to be scaled, new oceans to be navigated, new lands to be cultivated, and the zest and pleasure of it is always keen and fresh. We may envy the long-ago discoverers of islands and continents because of the delight afforded them, and may mournfully declare there are no more to find. But in the realms of mind there are wonder-worlds that stretch everywhere: we carry them locked in our brains, and if we will but batter down the barring doors we may enter those lands and sail those seas with the joy of true discoverers.

The nascent thought contains the power of a

continuous revelation as to moral obligation. Neglected duty produces spiritual callousness. The only way to get out of the darkness is to press toward the rising sun. To do one's duty to-day is a necessary step toward knowing it to-morrow. Those with faith in the race believe that the intuition of the hour is the surest guide to right doing. This statement is not meant to discredit careful judgment or to encourage rash action. Far from that; but the gist of the creed is that prompt action in moral conduct is, within itself, a great moral principle. Since truth is ab-solute, no man has a right to dicker with it. Delay causes doubts and fears to arise, while prompt action strengthens moral purpose. Even a trembling ethical judgment may be steadied by a bold step toward executing it. "One good turn deserves another," and it will have another, too. Good deeds follow each other.

A plantation in the wilderness is established by first cutting the forest trees from a small patch of land and there planting the grain. Around this opening more trees are cut the next year, and the pioneer's horizon is widened. Other grain is planted, and orchards and vineyards are set out. Upon the fruits of the cleared land the planter is able to sustain life and strength upon which to wage the battle against an ever-receding foe. Likewise, the nascent moral impulse is the seed first planted. It produces only as the originator removes obstacles to its growth. In this way a great moral establishment is founded, sustaining not only the life of its founder, but becoming a mighty factor for good in the lives of others.

The routine of moral duties tends to staleness. New enterprises are needed to give zest to one's convictions. One may hold certain ideals, theoretically, until it becomes a fixt habit not to put them into execution. Continuously running in old grooves makes religion conventional and formal. The spirit, smothered by words and forms, never has a chance to do a bit of spontaneous work. Little wonder that it pines and dies for want of exercise.

The nascent thought is a pioneer across the vast area of brain territory. Like the woodman of early colonial days, blazing the trees as he went through the forests, the new thought goes its way, leaving sure marks by which others may follow. If it be followed, a highway is established, and other thoughts come gliding smoothly into the beaten way; if not, the nascent thought wanders and dies alone, and the great forests of brain territory remain unexplored.

Two main causes keep the average brain from following up the trail of the new thought, *viz.*, indolence and fear. Thinking demands a great output of energy, and men shrink from it. This seems strange, seeing it is such delightful work, the most fascinating and remunerative that man ever enterprised. But a host of men who are not giving out any new thought, place themselves under strong suspicion that pure laziness is the preventing cause. This covers one class of non-producers. But are men afraid? It appears that they are. In all professions there are energetic men, those who demonstrate a desire to do their best, but who dread to launch out into ocean's deep, or to follow a straggling but bold thought into the rugged forest. That they are afraid is proven by the fact that all of their products are mediocre, tame, patterned after the work of others.

Nascent thoughts may be compared to sharpshooters who precede the rank and file of an army. Where they pass the main body can always go. But if the main body does not support these forerunners, they must surely perish. And the new thought must be supported at once. No parleying, no dallying is safe. The danger of being cut off is always imminent. But properly

followed up, a glorious conquest must be the result. All of the new territory is so much actual
gain added to the empire of kingly mind. Roads
are built as the army of the mind advances, sta-
tions are established, and the royal flag of thought
is unfurled over them.

The truth as to the mind's vastness does not
apply merely to the genius or colossus among his
fellows; it is of especial encouragement to the
mediocre man who has always felt keenly his
limitations. Even he has a brain so vast that he
can not utilize near all of its possibilities. There
are new languages for him to learn, new sciences
to master, world-enterprises to be launched. He
is a king, every inch of him, if he will but declare his kingship. His empire must be explored,
however, before it can be established. But if he
only presses his discoveries, diamond fields, richer
than those of Africa are before him; rose-gardens,
veritable Edens, lie in his way; nor does any
flaming sword prevent his entrance into them.
The rather has the guardian angel flung aside his
blade of death that he may entreat with out-
stretched hands all passing men to pause and
come within.

Chapter VIII

THE VITAL TOUCH

THE nascent thought logically suggests what I shall call the living touch. And it is not necessary to go very far to find a wholesome and practical illustration out of daily observation as to what I mean. For I have had an opportunity this very evening to note the renditions of half a dozen young women in their graduating exercises in music. I observed that one was exceedingly accurate as to technique, but too loud and harsh in touch; another lacked in technique and mechanical skill, manifesting a certain intractableness of spirit that was provoking to her masters, but pleasing to those that like boldness and independence. And yet a third, a timid, frail creature, with the usual slender fingers and liquid brown eyes, thrilled the audience, not only by her perfect skill in execution, but likewise with that strange tone-color of genius which she put into every note. I saw a lady in front of me, herself a musician, turn to her companion, and could but hear the excited whisper, "She has the living touch!"

Every one knows what that means, realizes that there is a difference, and is well aware that mere mechanical perfection does not touch the world's heart. The musician, like every other toiler in the human family, must put herself into her song if she expects it to thrill her hearers.

Apropos of the above, I knew a young minister who went to a great master of expression and said to him: "Sir, tell me, I pray, how I may speak with ease and effectiveness; for I find my throat growing tired, utterly fatigued in the delivery of a discourse. Worse still, my voice splits and creaks at times until my hearers seem to feel the pain and discomfort of my own suffering. I can not 'hold' my audience."

And that master of platform expression answered briefly: "Live your thoughts; speak only what you feel. Remember, as you stand before men, that you are a Living Voice."

Now, I consider that the master was uttering a true fundamental to a successful performance of any task, of any sort whatsoever. For it is not the lack of ability that makes so many fail, but the rather a lack of interest in what they perfunctorily do. One does not grow weary and bored in doing those things that one likes to do. And the world ever looks on with interest and delight at the doing of them in such a manner.

"I have been up a fortnight with my sick child," said a father to me. "I watched all through those nights myself, fearing to entrust him to another."

"You must have become painfully exhausted," I replied, sympathetically.

But his answer, given frankly, genuinely, filled me with amaze: "I never thought of myself; it was love for my boy, and anxiety for his life, that occupied my whole mind."

If we think of ourselves in a chronic manner, it follows of necessity that we shall grow weary. The living touch emanates from the life that is exuberant and abundant in its consecration to duty. I can not explain the depths of mystery in the tone-color of the voice, but I recognize it, feel it, am moved by it in the singer's words as she appears before her audience. Neither can I define the tone-color of an act, but I observe it in my own work and in that of others.

This living touch has to do with living things. And I fancy that the young woman who had the vital touch in the graduating recital somehow looked upon the great production which she rendered as being a living entity. It was not a matter of pressing the piano keys with her fingers in a marvelous fashion, but it was the far greater fact of meeting a living soul in the person of the famous composer of what she played, and that soul thrilled her own soul until hers responded into a glowing incandescence. And it was the light from the inner fires of her being that filled the music hall with glory.

I am sure that the performer in any sphere of activity needs to make out of his business something that lives by reason of human interest. That is, his work should be worthy of human interest because it touches the lives of human beings. And only as any work is of value to the race can there be any wholesome enthusiasm for it on the part of the doer. A man isolated forever from his fellows could not develop a large degree of interest in anything. The business world may talk in terms of railroads and steamships and factories until some pessimistic mind declares that the whole universe has run to materialism, and that the only voice that is heeded among men is the voice of the loom and shuttle, of wheels and whistles of industry. But, after all, it is the hum of human voices that makes the real hum in business: remove that, and the noise of machines would die out like the ticking of a run-down clock.

The foregoing is but a declaration that humanity and human industry are essentially identical; that work is only an expansion of man's self; that toil, in its dignified sense, is but a graphic exhibition of the heart. For me to separate myself from my task, and to think of it as being a distinct entity, is equivalent to despising the task; and that ever means failure in the performing of it. If my task is worth doing at all, it is worth loving with mind and heart. I am aware that this statement will be confronted forthwith by the retort that many of the pursuits of life are too trivial and common to dignify with one's affectionate pride. But just here is where we tremble on the brink of a precipice; we are in danger of falling into a huge abyss, in which the Master of Creation found the great world broken when He spoke about the small and common things of life. There was the lily, a very common flower, which nobody cared for; and He said, "Behold the lilies . . . Solomon in all his glory was not arrayed like one of these." And what does He mean? Certainly so much as this: even the tiny things of creation look beautiful to the Creator, who made them in the fulness of perfection.

And if it be a woman, sweeping the floor of a cottage, or a hen, in the shadows of the evening, calling her chirruping brood under her wings, there is always this meaning to the Master: the beauty, the glory, the sweetness of life, of duty. It is not what the duties of life are within themselves that make them common and onerous, but it is what one fails to put into them out of one's heart that leaves them ordinary; and, conversely, it is what one actually injects into them that lifts the most ordinary of performances into the third heaven, and crowns them with glory.

The tired man from his office goes out upon the golf-links and finds exhilaration and recreation in the game. Paradoxes logically follow; he returns home tired but rested; he has worked hard at playing, and now feels like more work. That great stove, the body, has burned up waste tissue very fast, and so, has built up the body with equal rapidity. Lastly, because the tired man has beaten his opponents on the links, he has laid by surplus force by which to beat his competitors in the game of business.

Interest in one's work means far more than interest from any financial investment one may possibly make. And as interest from an investment is continuous, so there should continuously leap out of one's work, springing up into one's heart, a stream of interest in that task which seems to the doer to be a fortune of untold value. No man should feel poor who has plenty to do and strength with which it may be enthusiastically done.

Here comes a youth, sauntering down life's great highway, and pausing, as he meets a friend, he declares with *ennui*: "I am only trying to kill a bit of time." O, crime of the centuries, sin of all sins, murder in the first degree—killing time! Kill an animal body and its skeleton remains; kill the oak, and its dead trunk still stands; burn down a mansion, and ashes are left with which the soil may be enriched; but kill Time and it is gone for ay, leaving not even a skeleton or trunk or fleck of ash. And to think that so precious a gift as time should hang with heaviness upon any mortal's hands, when it was given of the Creator to king and peasant alike as the one priceless treasure of the race!

Just the mere enjoyment of a sane, wholesome, clean physical existence is worth cultivating. As Browning has so finely exprest it:

"How good is man's life, the mere living! How fit to employ
All the heart and the soul and the senses forever in joy!"

But this exuberance is only basic to that deeper joy of the soul, in its living beauty, as it flowers out in the field of service. To feel, like the Master, that the virtue goes out of oneself, even tho the world but touches the hem of one's garment; to realize that one's hand can grasp the hand of the dead, and quicken the lifeless body into activity—that is joy, and that is service. And to have such a touch is the privilege of any human who is willing to enter the school of life with Jesus, the Carpenter, as Teacher. He studied life, as the "Principia" of all knowledge, and used naught but life-words in his terminology. And altho this greatest Teacher died while yet a young man, I find myself doubting if He ever would have become old in attitude had He lived twice or thrice as long. And this is only foundational to saying that there is a moral oughtness resting on us to remain young in spirit, not only for our own sakes but for the sake of others. For the true life-giver must ever be young.

Sad to relate, many who are young in years are old in attitude. For them there exists no wonderland. All of the joyous surprises of youth are gone. Why? Because the real life has oozed out of the heart, and wasted itself in the hot sands of some desert of ephemeral, sensuous passion. Life to them has lost its charm. Once the gardens were a-bloom, and the roses had burst out in red and white and gold; the violets had blossomed by the pathside, and the clematis had grown in gorgeous profusion over the figured trellises, while lilies of the valley nestled in many a sunny nook and smiled always. Youth loved these things of beauty and freshness, walked among them and carest them with great, wondering eyes of joy. And lo! the spirit of oldness seemed to fall upon the whole garden, while every green, blooming plant was nipt and deadened; and the soul, loitering down the pathways of forsaken youth, heard only the rustling of dry, lifeless leaves. Where lay the blame? In truth, it was the spirit of deadness that fell upon the heart, not the flowers; these are amaranthine in their freshness. The shame and blame is that those who may be young in body should become old in affection, old in their eager curiosity to know more of the unlimited truth of existence, and indifferent as to how abundant is the return that they may render out of their hearts to the great Giver of all life. We think of Wordsworth, that greatest of all of the mystic nature-poets, in those transcendent lines on the Immortality of the Soul, wherein he reached the mountain-top of inspiration, and saw with a spiritual vision that made the conventional life seem empty:

"There was a time when meadow, grove and stream,
 The earth and every common sight
 To me did seem
 Appareled in celestial light
 The glory and the freshness of a dream.
 It is not now as it hath been of yore;
 Turn whereso'er I may,
 By night or day
 The things which I have seen I now can see no more."

Now, wherein lies the sadness of this poet's statement? In that he at last has become disillusioned? Has come into a realization of things as they are? Surely not. For we ought to desire to know things as they exist, whether that knowledge brings pleasure or pain. If we are to live on the tinsel and glamor of appearances, let us die and be over with the farce of the present world. But the true ground of the lament inheres in the deplorable fact that the writer had ceased to see the real glory as it once imprest itself upon him, and which, to the perennially youthful mind must ever glow with its freshness. No one can exhaust the grandeur of a sunrise by enjoying it once, thrice, or a thousand times; for at the thousandth time it is just as full of mystery as it was at first.

It is the living touch that gives power to the prophet's prayers. Men pray "Our Father" until the words are repeated by the driest sort of rote. Not for much speaking are men heard in their supplications, but for the intensity and sincerity of their utterances. Man would as profitably set a graphophone going with entreaties to God as to speak words with his lips that do not arise, quivering with life, out of his soul.

The life-touch is merely a term to express articulation of my life with that of my neighbor, using the term neighbor in a racial sense. I am to feel the pain of all wrong in the earth, to experience the joy of all joy, to share with my brother all poverty and riches. Whatever burden I may carry is for the fraternity, and at the center of the world's work I must bury my heart.

Chapter IX

FAITH AND FOUNDATIONS

AN examination of foundations at this junc-
ture would seem naturally to articulate
itself with the preceding chapters and those that
are to follow. For, altho I may have chosen
the highest known standard of pitch in conduct,
whose vibrations a well-nigh infinite mind has
caught up, sympathetically; and even if, with
friendly attitude toward the universe that mind
has attacked its problems with an abiding passion, I feel the need in my spirit of having an
absolute assurance of my undergirdings. And
what would avail the efforts of a bold, independent mind, quivering with new-born life, if
that mind must impinge against an immovable
wall, called death? Or, if it must drop from
the shores of time down into an infinite abyss,
with no hope of a footing throughout eternity?

I am aware that in previous chapters it has
been assumed that there does exist a sure footing
for the immortal estate; but the human soul must
have more than this assumption; reason chal-

lenges all foregoing statements, and asks for proof according to its own standards of argument. And hence, I purpose to examine with some care certain essential elements that are basic to the perpetuity of any religion whatsoever. If the Christian religion can stand the test, my spirit will be satisfied with her outlook into the other world.

First of all, then, whence came our religion? How did we receive it? And the answer must admit that it is an inheritance. What we possess has been handed down to us in large measure from the past. It is no mere poetical fancy to declare myself the heir of all the ages; it is a substantial reality from which I could not escape if I would. No nation has ever come into possession, first-hand, of government, law or liberty. Nor has it created in any age a great literature or system of philosophy. It has been able to develop, add to what it has received, and thereby to enter upon some golden age of prosperity or intellectual achievement. But there never was a golden age that did not have beneath it the sterner iron age, since iron is necessary to beat out the gold; and there never was an iron age that did not have beneath it the stone age; for the stone age was the age of nature, and during that time man was taking a long course of instruction in laying foundations—and nature's distinctive foundations are in stone. It is true that there are ages in which something absolutely new seems to appear in certain branches of learning; but sufficient research reveals the fact that the veins of truth so appearing are only outcroppings of identical veins that run beneath the surface of some preceding age of civilization. There are at least intimations of every new field of discovery lying back somewhere in the past. It is the order of the universe that there should be an absolute unity in all plan and purpose. No man lives or dies to himself. When the Creator bade the race go forth and conquer the earth He instituted a cooperative association that was to spread with humanity around the world. The scattering of the nations at the Tower of Babel was only the setting of tribes to different tasks. Through different nationalities the lines of truth were to take divergent paths of direction, in order to traverse the entire range of human endeavor. These lines were to diverge so widely as to swing even into absolutely opposite directions to each other; but the order of the universe must be preserved, and the divergent lines must converge sometimes, somewhere. As sun rays come together through the medium of a converging lens, so the nations of the earth are to be brought together through the person of the Son of Man. That is the claim to be substantiated.

The law of cumulative inheritances is strikingly exemplified in the history of religion. Religions have risen and fallen, carrying up and down with them states and nations. But while a religion of a local or national scope has passed, religion, as a world-inheritance, has remained. Out of the fragments of every crumbled temple of religion, the race has picked up a gem of truth, a fleck of gold, and has carefully laid it away in the treasure-house of the centuries, from which is to be constructed the new and universal temple of God, "the house not made with hands," but made of the varied elements of all thought and effort of human kind.

The cause of the failure of any religion to abide, and to perpetuate the life of its adherents in a national existence, has arisen from the limitations of the truth it contained. Being only a partial revelation it of necessity had to fail. But while no good thing in religion has ever been lost, not all of the untruths of religion have passed away. Religion is stronger, more of a unit in this day than at any period in the race's history, and yet, there are many divergent lines that still refuse to be concentered into the One of eternity. The object of world-evangelization is to establish fully the law of spiritual economics, for God purposes gathering up all fragments of human effort and thought that "nothing be lost."

A distinctive testimony to the value of religion as a factor in unifying and developing a national life is, that every state has progressed hand-in-hand with its religion. When religion was strong, virile, vital, so was the state. There was never such a wholesome condition of national life during the history of the Roman state as in those early days when men believed in their gods, and in their power to help and bless them in war and peace. Then, the cooperation of their gods was necessary to success. But when the people lost faith in the gods, when they began to look upon them as myths and traditions, then it was the whole civilization began its decay for final passing. The purity of the family life went; with the dying of belief in the Penates, or household gods, the home began to deteriorate—there was no household god to look after it. In the days of faith in the Lares, or ancestral spirits, the home was pure and the hearthstone protected against invaders. With loss in that belief, however, the impurities from the outside crept in to vitiate the home purity and to destroy the sanctity of the home circle. Tacitus, in his "Germania," even before the empire had reached its greatest territorial extent, warns his countrymen against immorality, and the decadence of the sanctity of the family. He shows, by comparison, that the barbarous Germans are better, morally, than the cultured Romans. And all of this retrogression had been from what was originally a lofty plane of virtue, co-temporal with faith in religion. The time finally came when Roman writers, with barbed words, satirized the faith of the fathers.

A glance at more modern times only substantiates the argument that the integrity of a state is indissolubly linked with that of its prevailing religion. The middle of the eighteenth century found England in a most degraded condition, morally and politically. The Wesleyan revival, bringing to the masses a new faith in God, did much to save not only the Church, but the State as well.

But faith in God implies faith in the supernatural and, therefore, in the supra-rational. Rome's loss of faith in religion meant that, to the learned and cultivated, religion had sunk into a superstition bereft of every trace of the supernatural. And such an attitude could mean nothing less than a bald infidelity.

At a much later period in history, during the French Revolution, a complete repudiation of all that was supra-rational, could only mean a repudiation of all belief in God. And so, the "Age of Reason" had its birth. No mention of Deity was permitted in governmental documents. Reason, represented by a gaudily adorned female figure, was crowned and worshiped in the Notre Dame Cathedral. And France has not recovered from this shameless blasphemy to the Almighty to this day.

However, the passing Roman religion left a sacred deposit of faith in the Infinite, the supernatural. Religion, in form, had died, only to give place to a more vigorous and abiding type in the form of Christianity. True, the Christian faith had to find its first adherents among the poor and ignorant, since the educated class could not accept the belief in the resurrection of a crucified Redeemer. But this very fact—this supra-rational fact—which the Greeks laughed at when Paul preached at Athens, was the very element that appealed to the masses who had lost their gods. It was a joy to them to accept and honor a divine Christ.

What was true of the Roman religion in a limited sense, was true of the Jewish in a much larger degree. Jesus had declared that He had not come to destroy the religion, which He loved, but the rather to supplement and establish it. He, too, had to depend upon the ignorant and poor to accept His teaching; scribe and Pharisee were too humanly wise to adopt them.

But this utter dependence of religion upon the credence of the unlearned was in itself a strong credential to its supernatural element. They could not reason it all out, but to them that was a small thing, inasmuch as they were not by training sticklers for reason; it was enough that the new evangel appealed to their hearts, brought hope to their despairing souls. That was evidence enough to them that God was speaking.

On no other basis than that of the supernatural origin can one satisfactorily account for religion. To call it a human discovery, based on cunningly devised fables, foisted by priests upon the people in order to control them, is not to appeal to reason and the facts. Declaring it a sort of "pathological madness" does not satisfy the integrity of the intellect. Nor does the claim of George Eliot, that Christianity is merely a finely wrought-out system of utility, which the race has developed by experience, meet the demands of explanation. The fear of the elements, existing in the mind of primeval man, undoubtedly accounts for much of the religious emotion and many crude notions that prevailed among early nations and tribes. But this cold basis of reason as laid down in the theories of modern rationalists fails, since, logically, the foundation of fear would of necessity be destructive. Only love, and faith in a God of love, could produce the great constructive philosophy of Christianity. God, speaking to the heart of man, must have been the ultimate source of our religion. Nothing short of a divine origin, comparable to an ocean tide sweeping out across the plains of time, satisfies the mind as an efficient cause. Saint John speaks of a river of water, clear as crystal, proceeding "out of the throne of God and of the Lamb." That is religion of the abiding type. And when that tide touched this world in the dim dawn of creation, it was destined to flow on to the end of time. If the banks of the river in John's vision were lined with trees, bearing fruits, with leaves for the healing of the nations, the sacred trees and fruits and leaves have still remained as God's gift to men. And humanity has been fed out of this heavenly forest, has slaked its thirst from the crystal stream, too long to quit them. The trees are where the Creator planted them; man could not do it, tho he found them, and finding, has eaten and will ever eat of the fruits of his salvation.

The supernatural element in religion has preserved it from destruction, and this is preeminently true of the Christian faith. From the very birth of Christ to the present day every effort that an evil mind could conceive of has been instituted to destroy His religion. Herod endeavored to kill Him as a child, but failed. Later, the Jews did kill Him, only to enthrone Him forever in the hearts of the people. Then, as the Gospel spread, there arose a series of persecutions by the Roman state such as no religion except a God-nourished one could endure. The persecutions which the Jews instituted after the death of Jesus were eclipsed by those of the Roman emperor, Nero. The historian, Tacitus, tells of the rage that burned against the Christians. Followers of Christ were accused of having burned Rome, the evidence being that Nero himself had done it for amusement. Seeking to divert suspicion from himself, he began a series

of persecutions, the contemplation of which chills
the heart to this day. The believers were crucified, sewn up in skins of wild beasts and exposed
to the fury of dogs, and yet others covered with
combustible materials and used as torches to
light up the gardens of Nero. Under Domitian
the persecutions raged with redoubled fury, while
at the opening of the second century, with the re-
putedly humane Trajan on the throne, a fresh
onslaught was made upon the disciples of the
Nazarene. Pliny, proconsul of far-off Bithynia,
writes Trajan about these Christians, stating that
the only fault he could find in them was that
they were accustomed to meet before sunrise and
sing hymns of praise to Jesus as Deity! He
stated further that they then bound themselves
under solemn oath to commit no wickedness—
neither theft, nor robbery, nor adultery—and
never to break a promise. And they concluded
their simple worship by taking the Sacrament of
their Lord's last Supper on earth

Pliny proceeds to describe his method of deal-
ing with this strange sect. He demands that all
such believers shall repeat formulas of petitions
to the Roman gods, and to offer supplications,
with wine and frankincense, to the emperor's
image. If they did this blasphemy, they were

released; if not, executed. In reply to the proconsul's inquiry as to whether his method of
treatment were acceptable to the emperor, that
benign ruler speaks commendingly of his loyal
servant's mild measures!

We are left to infer from the historic facts in
the case that the gravamen of offense on the
part of these disciples of Jesus was that they believed in the divinity of their Lord, who had
risen from the dead, thus transcending all known
natural law. Strange as it may appear, the well-
meaning Marcus Aurelius, emperor in the latter
part of the second century, was relentless in his
hatred against Christians, many of whom perished at his behest. Passing over other reigns,
extending through another century, we pause a
moment to note the terrible persecutions under
Diocletian toward the close of the third century
of the Christian era. Never had blood of
martyrs flown so freely, the object of the state
being utterly to extirpate the new religion forever. The fury of the empire was carried to its
highest pitch of maddened frenzy because the
humble believers in the Nazarene attributed to
Him, as a risen Redeemer, powers that eclipsed
those which the vain rulers would arrogate to
themselves. It was the supremacy of Jesus that

offended them, just as it is His transcendent claim to divinity that offends the pride of my lord Man to-day.

To my mind nothing but the supernatural element in religion as taught by the Son of Man could survive the machinations of evil that were set for its destruction.

The supernatural element in Christianity can not be rationalized without destroying the religion itself in its true nature. That is, religion is dependent upon its supernatural element for its efficiency and perpetuity to the race, and the moment one has rationalized it, one finds it has melted away like the mists, in that its essential quality is discarded. Wherever reason has dissected and analyzed to a point of satisfactory explanation, religion takes leave as having no further mission to perform for man. Who cares for a religion that can not extend beyond the finite bounds of the human mind? The supra-rational in religion is precisely what has ever been attractive to the race. Efforts have not been wanting in any age to effect a rationalization of religious belief, altho rationalism, from the scientific standpoint is considered to have begun with Descartes. But the efforts of the Gnostics in the early days of the Church marked the utilization of the same ideas that arose about the middle of the eighteenth century, and in modern times have become well developed in certain phases of criticism. Neoplatonism, which began to flourish in the third century, represented a profound effort to rationalize the whole system of Christianity. Origen, the learned Alexandrian scholar and presbyter, was an apostle of this philosophy, which, in its final outcome, opened the way for Arianism, denying to Christ His divinity. The doctrines of Socinus, the Italian theologian, who lived in the sixteenth century, denied the essential unity of the Trinity, the divinity of Christ, and the atonement. These, and other teachings like them, mark out the path for all modern rationalism. The arguments of these Christian rationalizers sound strikingly like those of every modern rationalizer who, leaping up in ecstacy over his discoveries has cried, "Eureka!"

Now, why did the early Church reject these men and their philosophy? Essentially because to accept them would have meant death to the Church in its fundamental principles, connoting, as they do, supernatural sources.

This brings us to consider the paradox, namely, the reasonableness of a supra-rational religion. Of all religions, the Christian appeals to us as being the most wholesome for mind and body. But the human mind instinctively refuses to accept that which is irrational. No man can accept the non-rational and maintain his mental integrity and self-respect. The thinker naturally asks, Do you expect me to embrace a religion which, by its nature, is unreasonable? The answer must be an emphatic negative. God does not command the mind to stultify itself.

Let us hasten, however, to note that there is a vast difference between an irrational system of religion, and a religion which, in its ultimate reaches, is supra-rational. The Apostle Paul admirably expresses the intellectual basis of Christianity when he speaks of "the acknowledgment of the mystery of God, and the Father, and of Christ, in which (*i.e.*, in which acknowledgment) are hid all the treasures of wisdom and knowledge." (Col. 2 : 2-3.) That is, in the acceptance of the Gospel, the human mind acts in perfect accord with the laws of reason, in that it finds in this Gospel a philosophy of human life in its relation to the universe that is eminently satisfactory. In its comprehensible elements, the Gospel in an admirable manner satisfies both mind and heart, bringing peace to the soul. As to those higher mysteries, God and eternity, the heart can entrust itself to an Almighty One who is at the center of the universe, and who in Himself is a sufficient explanation of the unknowable. With perfect consistency the human mind can leave to God the solution of the insoluble; and any man is justifiable in flinging the burden of mystery upon a Creator who has redeemed him, and lifted him into a state of perfect peace, and of harmony with the world in which he finds himself.

The ancient Greeks believed that the gods lived on Mt. Olympus, and in that region held their councils relating to the destinies of men. Now, altho the Greeks could not scale Olympus, nor know the mysteries of those gods, they could explore the base of the mountain, be satisfied that its base was a part of the earth, and remain content to reap and sow their grain on the surrounding plains. So that the tangible and knowable was in some permanent and utilizable way linked with the intangible and unknowable. In like manner, the Christian trusts the God who is at the top of the mountain. There are, indeed, mysteries in the lofty, divine altitudes that he can not solve, but that limitation in no sense negates to his mind the realities of the mountain's base. Our Master Himself "went up into a mountain"

and was transfigured there, in the presence of
Moses and Elijah. His face was radiant as the
sun and His garments white as the light. The
disciples could not stand the vision, but falling
down hid their faces from the sight of that awful
mystery. They could not look upon Him there;
but when they came down from the mount they
could. For there, in the plain, the nimbus of
ineffable glory was vanished, and the supernal
whiteness and luster that had fallen from His
poor, seamless garb, left Him quite the picture of
the dust-covered pilgrim. Yet, He was the same
Lord, who had been transfigured; only, a part of
His glory had been left up in the mountain of
mysteries.

> "There are depths of love that I can not know
>   Till I cross the narrow sea,
> There are heights of joy that I may not reach
>   Till I rest in peace with Thee."

It is quite in keeping with this view of the
reasonableness of the Christian faith to note the
views of Descartes himself, the accredited founder
of modern rationalism. He went back of all accepted truth and philosophy until he reached a
good, clean spot upon which to stand, and where,
in open-mindedness, he might receive what of

truth came to him. Sifting out all known truth
and empiracle knowledge as being possibly faulty,
he laid down his familiar, "Cogito, ergo sum."
Accepting this, I therefore become certain of one
entity, namely, myself. But what of God? How
does an imperfect being come into the knowledge
of an infinitely perfect Being? Only in this way:
the idea of God must be innate, placed in the
mind by that perfect Being Himself, and so,
present because of the principle of construction of
the human mind. The principle of rationalism is
that the truth of a proposition must be tested by
its clear and distinct intelligibility; but inasmuch
as Descartes himself postulated God as a clear
induction according to the structure of the mind,
so is the principle for which I contend clearly
established, namely, the rationality of a supra-
rational religion. Its foundations are capable of
being scrutinized; one may look them over, investigate, analyze them. There is nothing in the
basic principles of Christianity that offends
normal reason. God is a reasonable postulate;
and with this postulate, we may easily conclude
that it was a logical act on the part of the Father
of men to come into the world in the form of a
Son, both divine and human, in order that He
might speak face to face with His brothers, and

tell them that the Father wanted them to come home.

But some one objects, You are violating your own premise, namely, that rationalization destroys religion. In reply, I make no denial that I am rationalizing, but I do it only to indicate the limitations of human reason, and to assert that the Gospel of Christ is the one power sufficient to redeem the soul. Moreover, the human mind, accepting the fundamental base of Christianity as rational, can, with consistency, commit itself to it as being a system which may be safely trusted, even when the light of reason fades out among the approaching shadows of death.

I have no hesitancy in declaring that the highest joy attainable is that which is found along the path of thought. Intellectual happiness is the purest and sweetest that can come to man. Physical sensations of taste and touch pass and become but a memory, having little pleasure in them. But the fruits of the joy of thinking abide. One can not forget them. The happiness of the traveler on the road of reason is sure as long as he keeps journeying. But just here I would say lies the need of the supra-rational element in man's religion, since the believer comes to a point in the road of reason beyond which he can not

proceed. It is then that there comes to his aid
that

> "Strong Son of God, immortal Love
> Whom we that have not seen Thy face,
> By faith, and faith alone embrace,
> Believing where we can not prove."

He takes man by the hand and leads him on.

Every student has had a taste of that feeling
of helplessness that surely comes to the intellectual
worker. I recall most distinctly my own sense of
disappointment as a young student of an "Introduction to Philosophy." I found the introduction so full of charm and promise that I could
scarcely wait; I was tempted to run ahead and
meet Philosophy before the author had brought
me face to face with her. It seemed to me that
if the introduction were so promising, Philosophy
herself would prove a panacea for all mental
aches and pains. And yet when I had met her,
I found that she was the rather a sphinx, pro-
posing, indeed, riddles of the universe, but leaving me to work out their meaning as best I could.
And withal, I found that there comes no explanation of the universe, this side of faith in a personal God, that is at all satisfactory. The human
mind at last reaches the topmost pinnacle of the
mountain. It is snow-capped, glistering in its

pure whiteness. But unless one has the companionship of the Unseen Personality, one must perish alone. How gladdening to the reason in these chilling regions, apart from "the maddening crowd," to find One clad in the transfigured garments of long ago, grasping tenderly the appealing hand, and saying, "Let not your heart be troubled: ye believe in God; believe also in Me."

But if the Christ bids the believer follow Him, how shall he do it? By standing upon the springboard of faith and leaping from that topmost crag of reason out into the sphere of spirit. There he finds himself outside the reach of earthly forces of gravitation, under the sway of law that reigns in the Universe of Spirit. And tending Godward, he lays his weary head upon the bosom of the Infinite, there to find eternal peace. It must all become clear then to the student; for the faith of man has become the reason of God; the supernatural in his religion has proven itself to be the reasoning of the Almighty. Such a state must be as intensely real to consciousness as ourselves. Instead of the supernatural becoming the offshoot of reason, we shall find that human rationalism is only a single ray of light that has fallen from the Sun of Righteousness upon the earth.

The attacks that have been made upon religion are, in their last analysis, the efforts of
rationalism to discredit the supra-rational. One
man, like Huxley, may question the integrity of
the Sacred Writings on the basis of the inac-
curacies of the old Usher chronology, while
another may make his attack upon the foundation
of inconsistency in the statement of fact. The
cruelties practised upon the Canaanites at the behest of Jehovah offer a reasonable cause for rejection of the divine scheme of leadership for a
different type of mind. These objections, along
with many others, are examples of mere logical
accidents. The largest contingent of doubters,
however, are rejecting the Scriptures on the
ground of questionable authenticity. I have no
desire at this point to inject any condemnation of
reverent students who are endeavoring to get the
most intelligent information possible as to the
authorship of the books of the Bible. All of
their efforts do a negligible amount of harm until
they begin to question the personality of God,
and His ability to speak to men. Since God
speaks to men through men, it would be very
natural for transcribers to make mistakes of
minor importance; but through all of the Sacred
Writings, the golden chain of truth runs, by

every logical test, and that truth is the expression of God to the race. And so, I repeat, all destructive criticism of the Bible and Christianity to-day springs from an abhorrence of God as a Person. Men may make attack upon the authenticity of certain biblical books, and I see no harm that may accrue eventually. But to question the authority of these books is a far different thing, involving a discrediting of internal evidence that is totally subversive of truth. That many errors have occurred in the many translations of the Scriptures no fair-minded student can reasonably doubt; but that the living chain that runs through them does not bind the world to a personal Creator is not apparent to the race, searching with open-mindedness for a sane philosophy of existence. Rationalism, as says Pfleiderer, does not object to the term *personal*, provided the rationalizer is permitted to define personality according to his own glossary. But the human heart replies: "I need no new definition of God, any more than I need to have the term father re-defined. I want a God who loves me, pities me, and who can help me when I come to Him in trouble."

Some day the supernatural will fade away and assume the familiar mien of the natural. There is no conflict in essence between nature and spirit; can be none. Only questions of human limitations are involved in the reconciliation between the two apparent contradictories. As already stated, the faith of man is but the reason of God at work through all the ages, for man and by man, lifting him more completely into the sway of spiritual forces. The final objective of faith is to interpret God through man, in terms of time and space, with a large margin of allowance for the border lines of infinity. This faith is, therefore, other-worldly in its nature above everything else ever conceived in human philosophy.

Looking down into the heart of humanity, and turning through the pages of God's revelation to men, we are imprest with two truths: man is unable to pull himself out of the slough of sin, and therefore, there must be some external force of infinite power to accomplish his salvation. And so radical must be man's change of nature that the process of his redemption is to involve an entirely new scheme in the history of God and His universe. At the center of this scheme stands the Cross, and this Cross represents the high-water mark of God's effort to complete man's creation; and it likewise represents the chief point of the revulsion of reason, as such, on the part of man. Since this Cross stands at the center of the mystery of all mysteries, we need not be amazed that the mind drew back from it. Saint Paul thinks of humanity as being dead in trespasses and sins (Col. 2:13-14). Christ forgives man's sin, quickens him into new life, and taking "the bond written in ordinances," nails it to the Cross, where it remains forever inoperative and annulled. Here, then, is mystery for us: a dead man, living a new life, with his sins in reality nailed to a Cross. The old order has passed. Jew and Greek have sinned, and in their sin they have conceived that no power can redeem a man out of his condition. And the wisdom of the ages rebels against the new scheme; there can be nothing to it. But those who are willing to hear, to listen, to see—to come and try its efficacy, find that the Cross becomes both power and wisdom.

According to the doctrines of Christ Himself, the redeemed man must begin at the bottom and work toward the top. That same minority of the race, which Matthew Arnold has said is the salvation of all governments, has ever been the saving instrumentality to religion. Only the few have accepted heartily the supernatural truth, making it a part of the fiber of their being.

And is it strange that the mighty in all ages have been unwilling to become as children in order to enter the Kingdom? It is a hard thing to repudiate all of one's foundations, and to begin over from the ground. And yet, the method is rational, at its core; for we "are children crying in the night"; man does need a Redeemer, must have one. And if man is willing to stoop low enough to reach childhood, the Redeemer is ready to lift him into a high and universal manhood, whose stature is measured in terms of Himself.

Much rationalizing has been done concerning the Cross, and much more will follow in the course of history. We may say with truth that the Cross of Jesus was the inevitable result of a clash of sin with goodness; we may think of it as a great, spectacular representation of the love of God, appealing to men—and it was all of that; nothing in history is at all comparable to it. And human reason goes further and declares that of all the crosses of history—and there have been thousands—there was none like His. Those other crosses—what of them? Good men and bad had died on them, crosses just as rugged and painful as His. And after Him, countless numbers of His countrymen died on crosses, writhing in death-agony, on hilltops, in public places, by the roadways. But these are all forgotten, unknown in history now as distinct figures. But His Cross stands out alone, "towering o'er the wrecks of time," seen of all the world. No civilized race on the globe that has not heard of that Cross; every detail connected with it is known; even the two thieves who died on crosses by Him are lifted into immortality because of that fact. For no artist could spread on canvas the Calvary scene without these other crosses, too, with their thieves upon them.

But rationalize all one may, there is a dizzy height to which one at last attains beyond which reason can not go, standing, as it does, in the presence of the Atonement, the vicarious sufferings of this High Priest of man, whose only sacrifice is that of His own body, meeting the needs of man's soul for all time. Then, like Thomas, the first Christian rationalizer, the finite reasoner lifts his voice and exclaims, "My Lord and my God!" And having proclaimed Him Lord, in recognition of His redeemership, a marvelous thing takes place without the aid of syllogism or logic: the reasoner finds that the Cross has become to him the power of God and His wisdom. That is, after an individual has bowed in submission before the Cross, he realizes that it has become the storm-center of human life by reason of the Christ who chose to die upon it. For the power of it is shown in that it lifts the individual out of the clutch of sin to a life of right living; the wisdom of it is declared in that it saves the fragments of a broken soul from destruction; and henceforth the redeemed slave becomes a mighty champion of the new evangel against all forces of evil.

The trend of thought in modern philosophy is that we can not go back of man's experience. The new pragmatism brushes aside the merely theoretical and gives place to practical results. A religion that is able to make bad men good, and good men better, must be the best religion.

I have likened the religion of Jesus to a stream of water, proceeding out from the throne of God and of the Lamb. It is flowing on, and must continue to flow. Men have tried to stop its current, but without avail. They may cause some disturbance in the waters, but it is the power of the waters that causes the ripple.

A large boulder lay in the bottom of the river which I knew in my boyhood. We called it the "big rock." And as it lifted its head, grim and dark, it created no small disturbance in the stream; but the river flowed on, not by reason of the power of the rock, but because the power was in the waters themselves. Objectors, likewise, to the supernatural Christ may seem to create some disturbance in the stream of Life; but the power lies in the Living Christ, not in themselves.

This same river would swell with rains and become a mighty flood, on whose bosom were borne logs and limbs and much debris, creating no small interest as they bounded along, seemingly a part of the waters. But they were not a part; somewhere the driftwood was flung out on a lonely shore and left to rot.

These illustrations are analogues of two classes of non-believers that are most prevalent: those who are positive objectors and try to stop the flow of the current; and the thoughtless, unconcerned, who follow in the stream of Christian civilization, who enjoy the benefits of religion, but are not in reality a part of the great movement. Flotsam and jetsam, the idle, thoughtless, and rationalistic—floating on the top like driftwood, or lying at the bottom like the rock, but never, in any sense, a part of the living stream.

To identify oneself with the living stream of water is to connect oneself with the universe.

For if I dip my hand in the spring from yonder hillside, I touch all oceans of the earth. If one drop of water were let fall into that streamlet, it would become a part of the whole system of seas and oceans. And if I become a living part of that stream proceeding out from the throne of God it will finally bear me back in its eternal circle to the place where it originated. I become an interpreter of the universe in terms of Christ. And looking joyously toward the final terminal, I may well say:

> "Sunset and evening star,
> And one clear call for me!
> And may there be no moaning of the bar
> When I put out to sea;
> But such a tide as moving seems asleep,
> Too full for sound and foam,
> When that which drew from out the boundless deep
> Turns again home."

Chapter X

THE LIFE MORE ABUNDANT

IF the statements of the preceding chapter are acceptable to reason, and if, therefore, we see fit to receive them as foundational for a philosophy of human existence, we must be tremendously imprest with the vastness of the field of endeavor that lies before us. For in their essential nature those statements have had to do with life as a force whose proper direction aims at an ultimate exploitation of all of the resources of the universe. Our chief purpose, then, should be the absorption and understanding of this principle. The task is most difficult.

"If life had described a single course, like that of a solid ball shot from a cannon, we should soon have been able to determine its direction," says Bergson (Creative Evolution, Chap. II). "But it proceeds rather like a shell," he continues, "which suddenly bursts into fragments, which fragments, being themselves shells, burst in their turn into fragments destined to burst again, and so on for a time incommensurably long."

That is, life, in its unfoldment, ever meets with resistance in the world of inert matter, and must struggle through it for a complete expression of itself. How long such a scheme of dualism must exist none can venture to assert, but the truth gleaned from such a philosophy is at least so much as this: life can not be imprisoned indefinitely by matter; for tho it be represt on the one side, it will break for freedom on another. It is as tho life had shackles upon her ankles, continuously retarding her progress toward the Infinite; but the Spirit of Life moves on, dragging the resisting ball and chain after her, much as the prisoner, pulling his heavy weights of clanging iron, moves forward despite the pain and anguish that he feels. And may I continue a step further in figure? Just as the bold convict now and again makes a dash for liberty, despite his heavy ball and chain, and the whizzing bullets of captors, and leaps, by half a miracle, into freedom, so does the Spirit of Life break from her bondage into the untrammeled sphere of a more abundant growth and expansion.

And I am not to complain of my captivity; since it exists, since it is a reality, I should take it as being the best channel through which I may come into the great new world that beckons me. Indeed, as I have said before, it is needful for me to cultivate even the friendly attitude toward resisting matter, and wring from it every secret that can be obtained, thus building up a new basis of eternal living.

But I am to keep distinctions in mind if I would not be ensnared. Matter helps to develop life, but it is not life; never can be. And so, my real self never is identical with what surrounds me; I am ever a living and distinct entity. My existence must ever be spiritual. The content of spirit must of necessity compose the sum of life's values. Outside of it there can be no high joy or deep sorrow, since within its boundaries alone may be found the objects and terms of interpretation possessing in any sense the nature of the final and absolute.

Joy that clusters around perishable goods can not be very deep, for the joy passes with the goods, or before they pass. Material objectives are painfully elusive, continuously changing shape and contour, even down through their molecular structures. The conclusion is inevitable: when the basis of joy disintegrates, the superstructure must take a hopeless fall.

Sorrow and disappointment, like joy, have their places in the soul realm. If trouble passes with the passing of material objects the thought would not be abhorrent. But the sad fact confronts us, that when physical shapes have changed and molecular bases have been broken up, these false gods fling back into the spiritual realm that which they can not support, and the mind, if unacquainted with any joy except that which clings to outward form, has no possession at all but the emptiness of sorrow and regret.

We all want joy—a statement fundamental to racial life. We must consider any man insincere who claims to have no desire for happiness. It must ever be the final goal of the heart. How obtain it? Where is it to be found?

The Son of Man makes this far-reaching claim: "I am come that ye might have life, and that ye might have it more abundantly." It is the abundant life that brings the real joy. Every one has, inherently, some traces of life, some rays of light emanating from the soul, but the source of the life and light in the superlative degree is God, consciously dwelling within.

Wherein consists the more abundant life, then? In disenthrallment, liberation, freedom. The most abhorrent bondage is that of mind. The war against human slavery has been so long and so persistent that it has finally disappeared from all civilized races. But the war against the bondage of the soul was declared afresh with the advent of the Man of Nazareth, who declared that he came to bring life in the place of death. His way of securing freedom to the soul was to open her doors to the larger realms of life.

I saw an orange plant growing in a jar. By and by the leaves began to turn to a sickly yellow, and it looked as if death to the little tree was imminent. The owner tapped the enclosing jar, whose restraining walls now fell away, displaying an intricate mass of roots that had been intercepted in their growth. The liberated prisoner was transplanted to the open ground where it might enjoy unrestrained freedom. It was only a few days until the change was evident; the myriad roots, drawing into their hungry mouths nourishment from the surrounding moist ground, sent up messages of hope and strength to the fading leaves, which began to throw aside their pallor of death for the rich, dark hue of living green. The abundant life had come by the breaking of prison barriers. It is surely the restraining walls built around human souls that the Master would break. For life is not to be considered as a sudden acquirement, as one would find a nugget of gold and become, in a twinkling, opulent. One may not leap from the deserts of death into some paradise of life with a single bound. The products of noble living come naturally, by gradual stages of development, enriching the receiver by daily increment.

Humanity suffers from surfeit, *ennui,* but this resultant does not obtain by reason of the quantity but rather of the quality of food forced upon the soul. If a man partakes of certain kinds of food he experiences an impoverishment, rather than an enrichment of blood. Some foods, of a frothy nature, have scant nourishment, while others, like bad mushrooms, vitiate and poison. The strength of a soul, taught by the Master of Life, lies in its discriminative power. There is about us continuously enough of poison to kill, if we only feed upon it. But there is enough of pure food to sustain and develop life if we but find and partake of it.

I see a water-lily lying yonder on the bosom of the lake. Its white petals are pure and clean, and yet, far down beneath, the lily's roots are growing in muck and ooze, foul and poisonous. But every mouth of the rootlets is wise: feeds only on compounds that will make the leaves above beautifully green, and the flower snowy white. Wonderful lily! Yet, not nearly so wonderful as I may be, if I but will, in discriminating between the pure and the impure elements of the world in which I live.

To continue the analogy of feeding and growth, one can but grant that the well-developed life is dependent upon a systematic method of securing nourishment and gaining strength. One of the many causes of failure lies in the use of spasmodic effort. The soul needs its breakfast as well as the body. A certain amount of stimulation and food is needed each day in order that the soul may have a healthy growth. I often reflect upon the wisdom of that prayer of the Psalmist when he entreated, "Cause me to hear thy loving kindness in the morning." If, when I awake, I can but translate the tramp of feet by my window, the chirp of bird in my big oak, the blast of the whistle from yonder factory, into the kindness of God, I have started well. Most likely I shall be able to transmute the jargon of the whole day into something gentler and kinder than the old hypersensitive nerves have been wont to allow in the past. The soul has gotten a good start, a correct setting in the beginning, so that all through the day it can draw its life from the elements in which it moves and lives. It goes "from strength to strength" in the day's tasks, grappling with the forces that oppose, just as the body meets the forces of the material world.

Life-fields lie about us, stretching in every direction toward the infinite. We are explorers in the vast fields, and our work is to advance as far as we may in search of new oceans and rivers and continents, laying claim to all we find as ours. It takes heroism to advance into the fields of life. I have seen the man who had been to Alaskan gold-fields. There he fought the elements, endured the hardships of the rigorous clime, searched for flecks of gold along the frozen streams, and came back, perhaps, with a neat bag of the precious metal. A certain amount of glamor surrounds this returned adventurer; for apart from the fact that he has gained wealth, he has suffered, displayed fortitude. Yet, I can not permit this conqueror of Alaska to be compared in heroism to the youth who sets out for rich gold-fields of the soul. He has heartaches, too; suffers the hardships of the explorer, the gloom of icy loneliness, the pain of toilsome search; but his wealth is beyond computation. Not only is he the world's grandest hero, but he is the possessor of the world's greatest riches. "A man's life consisteth not in the abundance of the things he possesseth." Why? Because the "things" are perishable; they vanish like the opalescent soapbubbles which children blow from pipes. They are pretty enough while they last, but they are gone so soon.

In that pathetic story that Guy de Maupassant tells of the lost necklace, one reads that for the one evening, at the brilliant ball, the necklace shone like real gems, and gave to its vain wearer quite a striking appearance. But the tragedy set in on the way home, when the false gems of paste began to melt and vanish, leaving the loser naught save a life of servility and toil by way of reparation to the owner. Ah, it is sad, but true as it is sorrowful, that any possession in the material realm will soon or late melt away from our grasp. In what does a man's life "consist," then? In *life*. Only as one can lay claim to life can one be sure of any value that is permanent, and only in life-fields can life be found.

The spirit of the seeker determines what he shall find. With a desire to find life, he can make discoveries in all fields of endeavor. To set out to find life in the abstract would be to pursue a will-o'-the-wisp, but to strive after it in business, science, literature, or the social sphere is quite feasible. The finding of life is realized only in some practical pursuit. All that a man learns and does may become aids in attaining unto what we call the imperishable goods. Two men acquire learning, the one a materialist, the other a life-seeker. In the end, the former has used up his possessions in seeing and hearing and eating and drinking, while the latter has only tapped the hidden springs of joy which flow on unceasingly, and with increased volume. The distinction between secular and Christian education consists in the very thing that I am endeavoring to emphasize, *viz.*, that any education that does not point beyond the realm of the physical, the plane of meat and bread, is secular, I do not care where it is taught; and all education that mounts above the physical and points with assurance to the world of spirit is essentially Christian. It may be taught in America or China, in the State university or Church college, but no matter where, it is really Christian if it opens up in the soul of the tutored a genuine desire for the invisible wealth of which the Master spoke when he referred to the "life more abundant."

The ideal set up in the life-more-abundant goal offers a marvelous paradox, for it hypothecates in humanity the qualities of both dreamer and actor. One of the dynamic truths of the new Christianity was that "young men should see visions and old men should dream dreams." One naturally thinks of a dreamer as lying very still, while the actor is generally viewed as a person not given to dreaming, scarcely taking time to idealize, but always in motion toward a goal. Both views are right to an extent; for men can not act while they dream, nor dream in acting. Yet, the truth of the paradox is evident, in that, with the life-seeker, activities follow dreams; for after strenuous movements on the field, a more productive realm is opened up for dreaming and vision-seeing. Reciprocal relations continuously exist between these factors in the great ideal, mutually strengthening each other. To bridge the chasm between dreams and completed acts is the finest of arts known to the race. Either without the other is totally inefficient in the attainment of the imperishable goods. The man who dreams, and executes not, ever becomes less practical, until finally he is lost in the confusing fogs of a hopeless unreality, while the visionless actor, in uprooting weeds and briers in God's garden, ruthlessly destroys many a sweet flower which the world sadly needs.

In order to make dreams live in action, the dreamer must have what is commonly called enthusiasm. Without it, any dream is as dead as the proverbial door-nail. I am aware that a good deal of sneering is indulged in against enthusiasm, because it is not essentially intellectual —and to be intellectual is one of the greatest desires of a proud mind. But, let me ask, what does intellectuality amount to apart from enthusiasm? Is it more than a mere dream itself? Profound interest in one's work will generally evolve enough intellectuality to accomplish its ends, while intellect, unaided by deep emotions of interest, will remain cold and unproductive. Nothing so fully supplies this needed ingredient for our work as a taste of the more abundant life, a real appreciation of its sweetness and content This appreciation of life can be gotten only by living it, really experiencing it. To live it, one must come into vital contact with the great Mind, with the Master, who said, "I come to bring life; I *am* life." A cultivation of acquaintanceship with Him ever brings with it the appreciation in question, the recognition of true values, by which one makes the first discoveries in the rich gold-fields of life. Then, with the discovery of gold, enthusiasm is sure to follow; for whoever, even in his dreams, discovered a pot of hidden treasure, and felt not the blood surge through his heart more swiftly?

This, therefore, I declare with all faith: he that once gets a taste of the real life will have more of it, even tho it involve the strenuous work of transforming the stuff composing dreams into substantial elements, the products of activities. The man void of enthusiasm and interest in life simply has no conception of what the true living is. He is ignorant of his own resources. While making appraisal of various values about him, he has totally failed to appraise with any accuracy the unlimited treasures hidden in his own soul. The more abundant life might be had by breaking an enclosing wall, and lo! he perishes like a fading pot-plant, with no kind hands to transplant it to a more fertile bed. He starves because he will not open his mouth for bread; he perishes, with the goblet full of the wine of life prest hard against his sealed lips.

Chapter XI

THE WORK OF THE SPIRIT

BUT granted the truth of every preceding assertion relating to the spiritual possibilities of man as the central figure in the new empire of life, the development of his potentialities is by no means capable of accomplishment excepting under yet another divine dispensation. Of what value is life to man unless he knows how to use and interpret it? A gold-seeker, wrecked upon the ocean, is embarrassed by the bag of precious metal which he tries to carry ashore. It would mean a fortune to him if he could safely land it; but it means death to him if he still clings to it. And yet again, there may be a formula for every known disease, if man but knew the right combination of the elements; but he will surely die with those very elements turned into enemies unless he knows how to mix them into a friendly combination. And equally true is it that the vast inheritance of life is of scant value to its possessor unless he knows the formulae by which it may be endlessly linked and continued. Mention has been made of the significant announcement of Jesus that He came to bring a more abundant life for the race. But His mission would have been futile if He had left the ignorant inheritor with no instrumentality of use and interpretation. He realizes that the language of life will be a strange tongue to men, and so He declares that He will send an Interpreter, whom He calls the Spirit of Truth. (John 15:26.) "It is expedient that I go away," He further declares. (John 16:7.) Why? That this Spirit of Truth might enable the race to use the life that it has inherited.

Brief reference has likewise been made to Saint Paul's declaration of this same Spirit's unutterable groaning and continuous intercession for man. (Rom. 8:26.) That is, God has not left the human heart alone, embarrassed by its very riches, weighted down in the wreckage of time by the abundance of wealth that it was unable to carry ashore. The Spirit's office is to supplement the scant strength of the distrest mariner, and to help him with his treasure to reach land. The Spirit of Truth is to help the soul construct a new world out of the myriad elements of Life, so that every new combination shall be essentially constructive. Without the guiding hand of this infinite Intelligence, even life combinations are negative and destructive, just as essentially good elements of matter are bad when wrongly combined.

The above premises certainly mean that the creation of man is still in progress, and that the Creator has yet greater things in mind to do for and in him. Realizing this fact, I have ever before me the possibility of becoming continuously a higher and truer type of being by utilizing the instrumentality that is mine as a gift.

I am living in a new world, that of Spirit. It is co-extensive with the world of life. Spirit is the language of life. If I can learn the language of Spirit I know how to speak in terms of life, and am assured of an ever-increasing dispensation of its riches.

The next great achievement of the race is that of acquiring the language of the Spirit. It is only by so doing that we may hope to become citizens of the larger universe. For as human language is a necessary acquirement for the cosmopolitan in the earth, so is divine language an essential to an understanding of God. Without the spoken word nations would deteriorate in all branches of enlightenment and civilization, becoming nothing more than mere physical organisms, living according to mechanical laws. But the spoken word makes the world's thought a common possession, which, with additions through the centuries, embraces the sum total of all knowledge. It links the race with itself for all time. In like manner, the language of Spirit, acquired by man, enables the learner to understand the nature of the Being that made him, and to learn from that Being His will and purposes. In short, the finite soul may, in prayer, communicate with the infinite Soul, and so, become more like Him.

It is true that there are many difficult language-forms that man finds it hard or impossible at the present to use; these he must leave to the Spirit who "makes intercession for him with groanings which can not be uttered." The entreaty must be made, the act of creation must proceed; and so, when man's lips become dumb God utters the entreaty to Himself for him, and when man's hands are strangely confused in completing his own creation, God rounds out the defective proportions for him.

If I were asked to give some concrete example of what I mean by the unmastered language of Spirit I should at once refer to the greatest joys and sorrows that come to our earthly lives. We have the joy of vision as we gaze upon a landscape, and words can not express it; tears of joy may spring to the eye, or, as Wordsworth says, there may be in the vision "thoughts too deep for tears." But the language of tears of joy is known to the Spirit. Likewise, an inexpressible sorrow, deeper than tears, may endeavor to utter its plaint in broken-hearted groans. But the Spirit knows well what they mean.

The philosophy of Jesus may be summed up in its relation to life in words like these: "He was the bringer of Life as an infinite and eternal inheritance, and the Spirit is the Transformer of human elements into a new and complete union with that Life." Man can fully express himself only as he has caught the Spirit of the Master. But having so done, he can utilize all natural forces and focalize them upon the one life-point until it blazes with the Divine illumination.

In the field of art, examples of what I mean may be found in abundance. Hegel has divided art into ancient, classic, and Christian. The first presents matter as being distinctly superior to spirit. Somewhere, beneath the mass of matter there may be spirit, but it is not only secondary to matter in its essential nature, but is, further-more, so totally eclipsed by overmastering materiality as to have but small play in its finite world.

Egyptian art offers a striking example of this type. Whether one pauses by the colossal pyramid, or lingers amid the ruins of some ancient temple, the same depressing sense of the supremacy of gross material elements chills the soul. There is in it all the discouraging attitude of the sphinx, whose face is stoically non-committal of any truth that lies buried in its stony heart. There may be a spirit somewhere beneath the surface, but the bare possibility leaves the investigating mind at a total loss as to how it may be found. The ultimate effect upon the observer is that of doubt and skepticism as to the reality of spirit in the first place; and in the second, if possibly the spirit may dwell within, it is conceived of as being unable to break through its enclosing shell.

Classic art, represented most strikingly by the Greeks, seems to recognize spirit in all of its development. But spirit, as an entity, never fully extricates itself from matter. In its efforts at disenthrallment, the prisoner never gets further than Prometheus, bound to the rock. Beauty and grace of form are always present, but these must ever display themselves in connection with the essentially earth-born element. Spirit, under such restraint, can never fully express herself. Tho she may lift the head of a god out of the grip of matter, his feet will drag as he rises, resounding with the clang of chains upon Olympus.

But Christian art, altho it may lose in some exquisite forms of beauty, does break away from matter, rising into the region of pure spirit. And once extricated, the Spirit of Christian art is in the sphere of universal freedom, possest of wings of Faith and Hope. The result of this highest type of art is the opening of the mind to the world of the Infinite, where an untrammeled imagination may build as high as it wills.

And the highest office of this highest type is that of making man into something finer and better than he has ever been. For, assuredly, the imagination never undertook so noble a task as that of constructing a new ideal of manhood. Every faculty of mind and heart has full play and liberty. And the wonderful possibilities thus accorded to a liberated mind, strongly connote the imperfections that have hitherto impeded the progress of the race. Man, as a factor in the material world, of which he is an essential part, has met defeat, since the very forces that he has corralled and harnessed have, in turn, overcome him. To leave him on a field of such doubtful conquest is to render any philosophy of life unsatisfactory and self-contradictory. On that field, man is a failure; give him the freedom of a liberated spirit, and he is a glorious success, a grand victory and triumph. The office of the Spirit is to perfect man into what he ought to be.

In this world of Spirit there is not only a new language, but a spiritualized counterpart of all material entities that are accounted of essential value by man. On no other basis of explanation would this earth be at all understandable. What is "Heaven" unless it represents such a spiritualization and unfoldment of all that is best in the world? And who would care to go there if he were assured he would find himself an utter stranger to all that he found?

Chapter XII

THE ENTITY OF CHARACTER

WE like the term "practical," and whatever system of thought, ethics or religion would appeal to man must demonstrate its right to be listed under this term. The race, as a whole, simply will not commit its hope to a system of truth that is so mixed with doubt as to render it largely guesswork.

In the immediately preceding chapter I have briefly set forth the philosophy of Jesus in its practical application to man's needs as a religious being. And in that doctrine I have declared the work of the Spirit to be essential for its fulfilment; without it, the message of the Nazarene to the world must have remained unheard; His evangel of hope must have died away for want of some one to carry it forward through the centuries. But now, in this busy twentieth century of ours, men will ask, Of what value is this work of the Spirit to us? Can it, and does it, meet our needs? In short, men want to know just what sort of concrete resultant is to come to them by the union of the Spirit with their own spirits. They would have something tangible; lay hold of a product that is a reality, and which can be considered as an asset of the soul.

In answer to such inquiries Christianity has to say that not only does the Spirit produce, in conjunction with man, a result that is an entity, but it is the most real and valuable entity of society and civilization, namely, character. What is there in literature or history that is more real to the thought of the world than that? Are the conquests of Napoleon any more real than the character of that genius? Does any man consider the achievements of Washington without continuously thinking of the character of the man that lay beneath and behind every act of patriotic service? I should say that the character of any citizen in a community is the real standard of appraisal by which that man is to be judged as a valuable or worthless asset to that community. Now, such a far-reaching premise as this being accepted, we may feel safe in saying that of all practical and beneficial processes going on in the world at this time, none is so much to be emphasized as that which builds up good character among the inhabitants.

Let us look into the process.   Somewhere

within my being there is a heart of action, a
motive-force of moral conduct. The Master has
likened this heart to a treasury, in which are de-
posited the possessions of an individual. It is
a repository of life's actions. Just as the precipitate falls to the bottom of the test-tube when
the proper re-agent is poured into the solution,
the gold and silver of moral values is flung down
into the repository of the heart as the result of
activities. Every day this process is going on and
every individual is gathering into himself certain
essential qualities which will determine whether
he is rich or poor, valuable or worthless to the
world. Not all precipitates in the laboratory are
of equal value; neither is every act of the individual of equal moral worth. Some acts are
strongly enough saturated with high moral quality
to render them noteworthy in the history of the
performers; others leave the actor changed but
little in riches or poverty. But so much is true:
There is, perhaps, no performance whatever in
the world of human intelligence that does not
either remotely or directly connote some ethical
quality. But it needs be said at this point also
that there exists a subtle danger of underestima-
ting or overestimating the moral worth of an individual upon the actual poverty or richness of a

single performance. Kings have been guilty of
deeds unworthy any degenerate in their realms,
while many a peasant has displayed nobility of
character worthy of royalty. It is true that a
saintly soul has, under trial, been stained by some
great sin, while a low-browed criminal has shown
a magnanimity on some rare occasion that won
the admiration of all the good. In either case,
it is difficult to appraise the striking example of
good or evil in the final estimate of character, at
its essential value.

It is palpable to every one, therefore, that the
filling of life's treasury involves the most complex activities known to the student of the soul.
Sometimes men do the unaccountable, even to
themselves. Wrong motives date back many
generations in their origin, and only omniscience
can sift out the compound responsibilities and
place them where they belong. Some unaccountable rudiment of a past age may, like the
vermiform appendix, assert itself at the most in-
opportune time, and from an absolutely unknown
cause. The inheritor of the rudiment has to
suffer from the very organ that was in a remote
age of service to his ancestors. Moral quality
in actions has changed radically during the centuries. It was a manly thing for my piratical

Viking antecedents to scour the seas in search of treasure that belonged to others. My German forebears were accustomed, with clear consciences, to use human skulls as drinking-cups from which they joyously quaffed the blood of their enemies. Such performances nowadays would be very reprehensible; but descendents of these barbarians are living to-day who take other people's property, and, in a figurative, yet terribly true sense, drink the blood of friend and foe alike. But who is able to judge these unfortunate inheritors except the Omniscient? Happily, we have inherited the unaccountable good impulse more abundantly than the bad. Some September zephyr, some lost chord of music, a spring bud or flower, or a snow-storm in winter may bring to the inheriting soul subtle suggestions and intuitions from long ago, telling it of the beauty of goodness. Anon the heart picks up a gem from the trash-pile of the centuries and finds within its crystal depths wondrous refractions of light from the face of the Son of Man who passed that way long, long ago.

The rustle of falling leaves in autumn days awakens in the soul strange longings after the Being whom the long-ago forest-men and cave-dwellers tried to find. Perhaps they endeavored to soften His anger by bloody human sacrifices, but their misconception of His nature has been slowly rectified through the centuries, and now, the modern soul has the nameless longing after Him, without that fearful dread and fear which haunted the cave-dweller. All of these intuitions, hopes, yearnings are the refinements of much rough ore melted in the crucible of time, and now that they are being strained out into pure gold the possessor can know its value by carrying it to the Assayer of the universe. It is ready to pass into the current coin of the Kingdom.

Let us be fair to our dual self, and revert to the painful fact that there is in the kingdom of the soul much of the counterfeit coin, a vast deal of brass that has not yet been filtered out. Slowly but surely the work of extricating has been done, but there is yet a staggering amount to do before we can declare that humanity as a whole connotes absolute values, with a standard karat of fineness stamped upon them. If autumn leaves, rustling to the earth, lure the soul back through centuries of divine intuitions after God, so does the freighted breeze from distant poppy-fields of sin overcome the heart with drowsiness and deadening anesthesia. Men are everywhere going astray under the stupefying effects of sin. The cumulative wrongs of the centuries are mysteriously piled at the door of unfortunate souls who lift their helpless hands appealingly to Heaven for help. Worse, some brutalized life, with seemingly more than its share of inherited evil, seems to glory in its bestiality.

Confronted by the inexorable law of Sinai which visits iniquity not only to the fourth but fortieth generation, we turn our eyes toward the eternal "hills whence cometh our help." We must be idealists to believe in the redemption of which I speak. We must take things as they are, and dream of them as they ought to be. Such an attitude makes real to us the best that man can hope. All of the combinations of noble soul-forces in the past are brought together in a new personality that ever tends toward the ideal. As the seventy-seven or more elements that make up the crust of our earth and its surrounding atmosphere form every compound that is both good and bad, so do the many inherited traits from the past compose the sum total of the race's goodness and badness. A good man has a predominance within him of compounded elements that are constructive, the evil man has a predominance of those that tend toward destruction.

All good and evil become, thereby, relative terms, for no man can yet claim the absolute in the good, nor be charged with being absolutely evil. But the tendency is the criterion that is to determine where the individual is to be placed. Judged by such a standard, the final destiny of man is capable of a continuous change, dependent upon his use or rejection of such help as may be proffered him by the Master of the universe of Spirit.

Left unaided the human soul could never eliminate from her complex self the elements that tend toward destruction. It is here that the Spirit, of whom Jesus prophesied, comes to the rescue of man, and demonstrates His mastery of destiny by a process of elimination. He becomes the re-agent, introduced into the life of the individual, and it is through the combination of human elements with Him that a new precipitate is thrown down from the complex solution. This resultant is a compound of positive goodness, made up of the divine and human agencies involved. This process, continued long enough, is destined to form the rich deposit of character, which is to be embodied in the superman of time and eternity. In this logical course of development, a real entity is evolved that is as much a fact of existence as a star or sun, and which, being spiritual, is more abiding. By this method, the spirit is filtering out the good elements, and leaving those that are useless; but the work is done with the cooperation and consent of the human factor. And this but means that the human will must determine its destiny in some large sense. "Let him that is righteous be righteous still; and let him that is filthy be filthy still." Unless the process of elimination is permitted, the refusing individual remains a chaotic mass of ill-assorted elements.

It is clear from the above conclusions that a good man is more than a mere tendency or potentiality—he is an actuality. For a good man is one who is not only disposed to do good acts, but who actually does them. A mere tendency toward goodness is by no means enough to lift man into the companionship of angels. Any man who is entitled to the encomium, "good," is one who has a character so positivized by the Spirit as to partake of the abiding nature of that Spirit. Such a character is undying, since its whole being is within the realm of life.

But while the character of the Christian is an entity, it is still filled with unrealized potentialities, so that "it doth not yet appear" what man shall be. Reverting to Bergson's figure of the exploding shell, this marvelous aggregation of vital forces into the entity of an individual character has within it dynamics enough to interest God forever. The constructive work of the Spirit expands toward the infinite as these exploding centers of life multiply themselves unceasingly. Instead of being something vague, indefinite, mystical, the Christian's character becomes the most meaningful term in the vocabulary of the race. It is not possible to destroy it; on the other hand, it is the one indestructible possession that man may carry out of one world into another. Character is not only immortal; it is immortality itself. Being the resultant of fusion of the spirit of man with the Spirit of God, Christian character must have the everlastingness of God.

Chapter XIII

THE VALUE OF A SOUL

SUCH a view of man as to his ultimate possibilities of development, forces us to the conclusion that we have never, in the history of the race, made an appraisal of the human soul that is at all commensurate with its value. If the individual, in his acquirement of a character possessing essentially divine elements in its content, is seemingly the sole survivor of all occupants and entities out of this world, we may logically conclude that the entire planet derives its meaning from man in the final reaches of his destiny. We could almost venture a step further and say, that so far as it is given us to know, humanity is the exponent of the entire universe, and that as man is lifted into an expression of the power of that exponent he is accompanied by the Spirit along an infinite path. For man assuredly touches all earthly elements with a shaping hand, and in some considerable sense lays tribute upon stars, planets and satellites of the expanded universe. For he can not till the soil without taking knowledge of the sun, nor sail the seas without the guidance of the stars. He is linked by the law of destiny to the greatest as well as the smallest things.

In the light of such a sweeping connotation of the term *man,* it is startling to reflect upon the trivial consideration that has been given to human life in the past, and which, in many respects, is still accorded it. The very greatest of the earlier civilizations cared little that man suffered, starved, died. Human slavery, within the recollection of the present age, was viewed as a matter of no concern. The superiority of one race to another was asserted upon the basis of religious conviction. The butcheries of the middle ages under the guise of religion showed a total lack in valuation of human life. The anomaly of religion, intended for man's uplift, being used to crush him, still fills the observer with wonder, as he follows the course of conflicts through long centuries. War, with its bloodshed, atrocities, destruction to life and property, has ever been an insult to the Almighty.

Napoleon, during the famous Moscow campaign, was riding over the bloody field of Smolensk with one of his marshals. The French had been victorious, and the loyal lieutenant of the great conqueror exclaimed: "A great victory, Sire, but made at a tremendous cost."

"Ah!" scornfully ejaculated the Emperor, "you can not make an omelette without breaking a few eggs."

A wounded Frenchman, lying on the ground, heard his adored ruler speak thus slightingly of the slaughter of his fellow soldiers. Years after the battle of Waterloo had been fought, this same soldier, having survived the sufferings of that terrible invasion of Russia, was giving an account of his sensations and reflections as he lay on the field of Smolensk and heard the flippant comment of the world-conqueror concerning human life.

"I had ever idolized him," declared he, "but my idol was crusht and broken there. In my own mind I foresaw the sinking of the star of Napoleon was a matter of fate."

If the Corsican had but imbibed the revolutionary teachings of the Nazarene, he would never have thought thus of life as being a mere tool with which to carve out empires and destroy kingdoms. The career of Napoleon had its beginning in an upheaval of political conditions that lured the colossal genius of warfare toward a course of self-aggrandizement terminating in his final downfall; but the future of Jesus took its direction from a different type of upheaval, having to do with the soul-life of the race. Every parable that He spoke was revolutionary in its tendency. And it is but logical that He, following the trend of His teachings, should realize an infinite expansion of ideal and life involved in them. Jesus is at home when discussing anything that relates to man's destiny. What He might have said of things or principles in the abstract, had He so willed, I do not venture to assert. But this I do declare with full conviction: He never exprest Himself in abstract terms during His earthly career. And whatever He said about material things was only by way of illustrating the matchless worth of an individual. He deprecated above all things the loss of life, as belonging to man, and it is in keeping with such a principle that He spent so much of His time in the healing of disease.

But the teachings of Jesus went far deeper than a mere respect for, and sympathy with, life as only an entity of the Creator's Kingdom. He declared the foundations of the Kingdom were based upon child-life. The life of a human being in its beginning is at the center of God's universe. And whatever man becomes is only an expansion, a development, of this life as it came out from the Creator's Self. Wordsworth expresses it:

"Our birth is but a sleep and a forgetting:
The Soul that rises with us, our life's Star,
Hath had elsewhere its setting;
And cometh from afar:
Not in entire forgetfulness,
And not in utter nakedness,
But trailing clouds of glory do we come
From God, who is our home:
Heaven lies about us in our *infancy!*"

It is, then, the beginnings of life that make man of value; his source, origin, make his destiny of significance. And Jesus expends all of the mighty forces of His being in breaking the walls of the "prison-house" that have grown around the developing youth and mature man, in order that the prisoner might "see the light and whence it flows." The sacredness of human life can be realized only as it is conceived of as coming directly from God.

The history of Jesus is one prolonged answer to the old-time inquiry, What is man? And the sacrifice of His body vicariously is a declaration that man is the dearest object of God's creation, that he is a child of the Almighty. Such a revolutionary concept of humanity has, of necessity, been long in its unfoldment, and is yet to be

grasped in its fulness. For according to its essential meaning, a human life is too sacred to be
abused, maltreated, or scorned. Such a view
opens the way for the most profound constructive
philosophy of humanity, being foundational to all
modern social work looking toward protecting,
conserving and developing the individual. Men
stand condemned by their own consciousness of
divine origin as they behold the squalor, poverty
and ignorance of the majority of their brothers
and sisters. It is not going too far to say that
the housing conditions of a large portion of the
laboring class are an insult to the Almighty, since
those conditions are unsanitary and unfavorable
to the development of a sense of dignity and self-
respect. If a tenement owner allows occupants
of his properties to be huddled up in quarters
where it is not only impossible to keep clean, but
difficult to keep virtuous, can such an owner have
the spirit of Jesus, who placed the Child in the
midst of the kingdom, and begged for him the consideration of the world? And yet, taking as an
example, the cities of the South, where are
gathered hordes of the negro population, we find
housing conditions decidedly unfavorable to
physical well-being and moral development. It
is well known to every student of such conditions

that very few of the tenements occupied by this class are provided with sufficient bathing and other facilities for health and cleanliness. Families are crowded together in a manner that makes the conserving of family purity among the intermingling families almost impossible.

The truth of the above statements emphasizes, as Heaven-imposed, the duty of every landlord to build such houses as shall render it easier for the tenant to bring up his children with a measure of decency. And the day must come when it shall be considered a heinous social sin to erect any other class of tenements.

I like to think of Jesus as being the great Leader of the people. I consider that the Son of Man was never so serenely satisfied as when He was leading a great multitude out into the countryside, there to speak to them out of an affectionate soul. They were motley, ignorant, untidy, ill-fed and ill-clad, but they were human beings, and it was His mission to touch their lives in that deep, personal way that would convince them of His friendship. He saw them sick, and healed them; recognized their hunger, and fed them. And whatever men may think of the miracles of the loaves and fishes, whereby this hungry rabble was sometimes fed, we may be sure that to One who loved the multitude nothing could have been more appealing than the act of feeding them. To Him it was such a sacred object—a body of human flesh, no matter how badly it was appareled, just because it was the house—the tenement—in which one of His brothers lived. Because of His valuation of this body, He could conceive of no social duty so high as this—love thy neighbor as thyself.

And this second of the commandments offers a new ground of appraisal for oneself. For to love my neighbor as myself means that the norm of my attitude toward the whole world is the attitude which I bear to myself. I am indissolubly linked to my fellows. And this does not mean that I am to be a self-centered egotist, a conceited and puffed-up soul; for to appreciate myself is to recognize my true value, to know just what I am worth. It is just as wrong, from the viewpoint of the divine economics, to undervalue as to overvalue my resources. The one is on a parity with returning property below its value in order to escape just taxation; the other is comparable to watering securities to the deception of those who would buy. A fair and just return before the tribunal of conscience of what my individual soul is worth is necessary if I would correctly appraise the worth of other souls. God's system of economics demands that we should link ourselves together on a common ground of brotherhood, looking toward the saving of all human values, since they are so immeasurably precious. According to this standard, no man can pray for himself without groaning in spirit for the uplift and redemption of others, and no scheme of his life is unselfish unless it ever considers its effect upon other members of the race.

This recognition of the value of human life is absolutely necessary to the accomplishment of great things. Self-confidence is only self-valuation, and whatever is called self-confidence without the basis of true valuation is mere folly. George Eliot, with all of her virility of mind, was late in beginning her work simply because she had no confidence in her ability. The resources were there, but she did not believe in them. With the growth of her estimate of her soul-forces she developed a confidence in her ability to utilize them. And this leads me to say that all genuine recognition of soul-values must be followed by a realization of them. It simply can not be otherwise. The Son of Man had such faith in His kingdom as to liken it to a gem, hid in a field, which, when a man had discovered, he bought at the cost of his entire possessions.

Much pain and hardship is to be undergone, it is true, if one would exploit the resources of one's soul. To find the hidden gems of earth much toil must be expended in digging and sifting. Likewise, to pull up out of the soil its rich potentialities into food-compounds there must be much clearing of ground, digging up of stumps and roots, breaking and pulverizing of rocks. But the harvests that result make all pain and toil seem as naught. For if I can "come to myself"— realize upon my assets—see myself, face to face— I am immeasurably rich.

And the while I am realizing myself, I am helping others to realize themselves, both materially and spiritually. Whoever makes bread more plentiful is a true brother to man, and he that opens up the treasures of spiritual riches to his fellows has tasted the joy of being neighborly.

Chapter XIV

IN THE SMITHY OF GOD

I HAVE mentioned the love of Jesus for the multitude, and I would revert again to the deep compassion which the masses aroused in His soul. "And when He saw the multitudes, He was moved with compassion on them," indicates more than a passing whim, superficial sentimentalism, professional charity on His part. A great wave of pathos and heart-sickening sorrow swept over His soul. One looks upon a horrible accident, sees a life mangled and crusht under cruel wheels, and feels the sensation as if the heart were melting; paleness is written upon the observer's face, and he reels into unconsciousness, perhaps, under the shock of the vision of a broken body. Such was the sense of pity that Jesus had as He saw the multitude, "because they fainted, and were scattered abroad, as sheep having no shepherd." That is, these people were as a flock of sheep, flayed and skinned, torn by briers and thorns, bleeding from the teeth of wolves, unshepherded, uncared for. And for that reason,

He was moved almost to fainting. These people had been exploited by robbers and thieves, elbowed from places in which to work out the bread problem. They had no chance. And it is here that Jesus anticipates the industrial problems of all ages. He is concerned in the masses, as a whole.

It was not an abstraction with Him, as with Emerson, who is quoted as saying, "I like man, not men." Concretely, the Son of Man cared for the crowd, with all of its unloveliness, dirt, squalor, snarling and snapping. Why? Because, economically, the crowd holds within itself the aggregate wealth of the spiritual universe.

But the Master was no mere dreamer. Keeping before Him always the vision of the multitude, He turned the emotions aroused into focalized effect upon the individual. He never allowed the mass-effect of the many to divert His mind from attention to the one. For that one must ever be the leavening unit of the crowd.

To talk to the masses is much easier than to talk to the individual. One gets only a panorama of the former; but with the latter, there must be a face-to-face view, a looking of one soul down into the depths of another soul. Jesus kept an even balance between the two effects. He allowed nothing to come between Him and the individual. And for this reason He seemed often to repress Himself as He discoursed of living, growing things in the material world. The poet could almost wish that Jesus had said more about the growing lilies: what a beautiful piece of literature it would have been for all ages! And why did He not say more of the corn-fields, with their rustling blades and ripening ears? Not because He did not appreciate their beauty, I must think; the few touches of the artist here and there in His parables show that He recognized the beautiful in everything. But His philosophy of life demanded that even a lily or a stalk of corn had only one mission—to make manhood. All plant and animal growths are useful as vehicles upon which man may be transported to his destiny. There are some sixteen elements composing the human body, but they can not enter the system in a crude, raw state and be utilized by the digestion for muscle-building. They must be pulled up in large measure by the plants, and so mixed and combined as to make them wholesome to the human species. Or, these plants are consumed by lower animals upon which man feeds, and finally reach the human body, ready for nerve, bone, and tissue. Man's body becomes, then, a great refinery, in which all crude elements are transformed into the finest output of creation.

By this process we realize that God is continuously creating men according to the formula of the centuries. Man becomes God's refined being, having been carried through many fires and laboratories. He loses something, it is true; for man can not have all of the sweetness of the lily, the peculiar glory of the corn-fields, the strength of the lion and tiger. "There is one glory of the sun, and another glory of the moon, and another glory of the stars." But man gets the best for himself, by the process of elimination and absorption, that the Creator has determined for him.

And since God has been willing to make such a tremendous outlay in nature for the benefit of man, and for his final development, it is no marvel that Jesus declared God's love for man to be greater than His love for birds and flowers. And we would reasonably expect Jesus to concentrate His chief attention upon humanity, rather than upon "nature" and the surrounding world. The material world becomes only a medium through which life flows, like an ocean-tide, sweeping on in resistless power. The life oozes through, like water percolating through desert sands, finally breaking into the individual stream called *man*. More: the divergent currents break yet again into great divisions which are racial, and we have the divisions of white, black, yellow, brown, and bronze peoples. These all have brought the pigments of color with them as they have passed through the great refinery, the circumstances and environments all being of the Creator's own shaping. And so, circumstance and environment become a part of God's method in the completion of man's creation.

I have indicated the kind of regard the Creator has for His birds and plants. Surely He stoops to caress the wild violet and daisy oftentimes. But He never neglected a man for a flower yet; never will for a moment fail in His first love, the Child of Creation. And it grieves the heart of the Creator to see this favorite, man, forgetting his own bigger destiny in an overfond admiration for flower-beds. One seems so near to God when one is surrounded by the roses of a sunny garden that the temptation is to lay down one's staff and say, Here let me live and die, among the sweets of the Almighty! It seems to be in keeping with the most artistic, refined and cultured life to remain there for all time. Likewise, men pitch their tents by the bake-shop and tailor-shop and say, This is a good place to spend my days. And it does seem to be well enough to the superficial mind; and reasons for feeding and decorating the body are so specious that the wisest of men must beware lest they become confused thereby. But the Master ever inquires, "Is not the life more than meat and the body than raiment?" Surely, even the physical organism must have a higher destiny than that of mere food and covering. I often reflect upon that unfortunate soul which the ejected evil spirit found, on his return, "Empty, swept and garnished." Sad enough to be empty and swept, but worst of all is it to be garnished! For that term signifies decorated, adorned, beautified, with all of the garments and trappings of time that would make a physical being beautiful. And what is it in even these decorations to cause sadness? Surely something like this: these adornments, like the wreaths of some festal day, soon wither and then all is gone. Think of a human soul, all covered over and bedecked with roses; it looks beautiful for one day, and seems a-thrill with life and freshness. But to-morrow, the covering of beauty is dead, and the soul is naked, and unlovely in its barrenness.

The grief to the Creator arises, not from the

use of His things of beauty and utility, but from the abuse of them. Men are perfectly justifiable in admiring everything of beauty, and even in wearing perishable garlands. But these are only incidental to the soul's triumphal march to the Kingdom, even as the palm-branches strewn in the King's path were incidental to His entry into Jerusalem on that glad day when multitudes cried, "Hosanna! Blessed is he that cometh in the name of the Lord." The empire of the soul can never inhere in anything that fades or grows old or dies. And when these perishable goods intervene between the soul and God, it means the clogging of the stream of life in its onward flow; it is like blocking the highway on which the heart travels, and compelling it to forego the joy of reaching the eternal city, the capital city of the finest affections and desires of the immortal self.

All matter belongs to God, and out of it He has made a great smithy where the elements of manhood are better welded. He wields the sledge-hammer, watches with interest and sympathy the sparks as they fly. The soul of man turns and groans in the glowing fires, fanned by the breath of the Almighty. He looks down into the blazing soul, at its white heat of passion and suffering, and with great compassion fixes His gaze upon it until, lo! His eternal image is caught by the molten elements and congealed into an abiding likeness that makes man the chosen child of Heaven. Henceforth, the offspring knows its Father, by highest intuition, *feeling,* rather than *seeing* Him.

But the soul must travel through the world of matter before it can come face to face with Him. Sir Oliver Lodge has said: "The boundary between the two states—the known and the unknown—is still substantial, but it is wearing thin in places; and like excavators engaged in boring a tunnel from opposite ends, amid the roar of water and other noises, we are beginning to hear now and again the strokes of the pickaxes of our comrades on the other side." We are working on this side, and the liberated forces of the race are working on the other side. God is with both sides, and He will be at the meeting-point, when the two rush together in tumultuous joy.

Chapter XV

THE QUEST FOR PERFECTION

NO man that ever lived had such an understanding of the sins of the race as did Jesus of Nazareth. He saw the sin of the world in its most vicious and revengeful forms, realized the death of its bite and the poison of its sting. He saw man at his worst oftener than at his best. Never did prophet or seer have less to encourage him than did Jesus. But persecution and crucifixion could not chill His sympathy for the multitude, whom He loved and prayed for to the bitter end. And even in the glory of His greatest triumphs, He felt a compassion for the masses, as stated in the foregoing pages, that had in it the sensation of swooning, dying.

But if the Son of Man saw the sins of the race as none other ever had, so did He see the possibilities of the human soul as no prophet had been able to see them, even in his most optimistic mood. Jesus had faith in man and in the final outcome of his destiny despite his ingratitude, unbelief, and crime. Leverrier, noticing the aberrations in the planetary system, declared that there must be yet another planet. So sure was he of his conclusions that he covered with his telescope the path of the oncoming orb and made the discovery of Neptune. It was in such a spirit that Jesus was willing to await the approach along the orbit of the race the new man, redeemed from the power of evil. He knew that some time man *must* swing into the light of a new Heaven and a new earth.

And the waiting of Jesus was by the orbit of a path that would lead man not only out of sin but unto perfection. Herein He demonstrated a faith that even now staggers and puzzles the souls of men. It seems hard enough to conceive of finite, sinful man as being saved from the evil, but to bespeak for him a salvation that leads to a perfect state seems too idealistic. But Jesus is essentially an idealist, and nothing, to His mind, can loom up as an obstacle between man and God sufficiently great to stop the progress of a Heaven-bent soul. God is perfect, and any being that approaches Him must be perfect. Therefore, Jesus calls the race to perfection in terms that can not be gainsaid, altho they must be dwelt upon in order to be understood.

What sort of a perfection then is man called upon to strive after? That which would be commensurate in its scope with that of God? To make such a claim would be folly. The perfection can be only that of a human being. Man may lawfully strive after the perfection of his kind, and so may aspire to be a perfect son of God. But this does not mean to be God; there is a difference between sonship and eternal Fatherhood as wide as that existing between finite and Infinite. But to be a perfect man opens before the aspirant a path of infinite length; he must ever be a traveler on that way if he would comply with the Master's injunction, "Be ye perfect."

Man is enjoined, then, to strive after a perfection that reaches the highest interpretation of the particular age in which he lives. The race is ever moving from darkness into a clearer twilight. There is a social conscience to be recognized which is but the accumulation of every increment of power from age to age. The twentieth century man must have within him a compound of all of the best elements of the nineteen centuries; yea, of all the centuries that have preceded him. If he is true to the laws of eternal progress, the last man to quit the shores of time must be the best.

Meantime, false standards are continuously being set up by many, and they all have their adherents. There is much of the polite society of the age that does not demand a pure life. Irreverence is rife, divorce laws have become lax, places of evil are winked at as being necessary. And the sophist glibly reasons that whatever is necessary is, essentially, right, the argument leading its champion not merely at a tangent from the true course, but actually forcing him to double back upon a track that leads him into the darkest ages of the past. The difficulty all arises from an acceptance of the wrong premise, instead of the idealism of Jesus.

It is necessary for the progressive Christian to clash in ideal continuously with certain moral and religious reactionaries, just as the Founder of his faith clashed unto the death with the reactionaries of His age. The advancing Christian, then, seems to his opposers to be living ahead of his age so far as to be impractical; he is ridiculed as being a crank, or treated with disdain as a mystic. The weapon of ridicule is the last resort of those who are against holy living and pure thinking.

At the center of progressive religion there lives the fundamental principle of moral restraint and self-control. Perfection is attainable not merely by lopping off evil tendencies, but also by a constant development of rudiments of goodness. The gospel of Jesus calls for the sacrifice of many desires. No matter how much money, or education, or culture one has obtained, the need still exists of throwing aside weights in order that the soul may speed all the faster along the orbit of life and truth. And since the process of elimination of evil is an endless one, the ideal of perfection ever recedes as the soul moves on. New discoveries of unused potentialities come into view as the litter and debris of the false are cleared away from soul-fields. And the idealist finds that it is not enough merely to avoid presumptuous sins, but that the demand of Heaven is for a constant increase in positive goodness. In the sense of using all of his powers to do good, the Christian finds that he is still, ever, always lacking; he remains a sinner by omission. As the energy of earth, air and sunshine are continuously unused in their full extent, so the idealist finds that there is a flood of light and life poured down upon him from on high which is not utilized.

Not only, then, is the Christian called to such a perfection as is interpreted by the highest living of his age, but he is urged to that far-away perfection which may be only dimly descried by his imagination; he must live according to the standards of the unknown. Urged on by the powerful rightness of such a moral paradox, man realizes that his peace of soul lies in pressing toward the acquirement of something that he does not possess. Every sane ideal of life is capable of being incarnated. And this potentiality throws an equal burden of responsibility upon every heart which, in its most exalted moments of spirituality, aspires after the most precious states of the imagined world. The good man is constantly urged toward being a better man, and this better man is prest in spirit to strive after perfection. The soul of such a being passes the stage of joyous triumph upon the mere overcoming of gross temptations, or even of complete mastery over the body; the time comes when the illumined spirit is ecstatic only in the atmosphere of a pure imagination. Such an ideal forecasts a time when every soul having even an impure thought will don sackcloth as becoming garb for its sinfulness.

It is only by such a positive and far-reaching idealism that the Christian can substantiate his claim to authority based upon the supernatural. For if he is willing to conform to the standards of the natural, his system of ethics has no better chance of triumph than any of a score of other systems. He must insist that his scheme of life demands that every thought or imagination of the mind must pass in review before the tribunal of the Absolute. The nearest and dearest object of his fleshly desires must be "plucked out" of his life if it be found to intervene between him and the Perfect One. He is to find his superiority to all other systems by bending low in the valley of humiliation and by bestowing love upon even those that are hateful. His life is to be a continuous and living sacrifice, since his Master based His entire system of truth upon that principle.

I am aware that such an ideal strains the nerves of even the most consecrated soul. But whoever follows the career of the Captain of Salvation must concede that it was ever in His mind. One thinks of Walt Whitman:

> "O Captain! my Captain!
> Our fearful trip is done;
> The ship has weathered every rack,
> The prize we sought is won.
> The port is near, the bells I hear,
> The people all exulting,
> While follow eyes the steady keel,
> The vessel grim and daring.
> But O heart! heart! heart!
> O the bleeding drops of red,
> Where on the deck my Captain lies,
> Fallen, cold and dead."

These lines, athrill with exalted pathos, were

applied by Whitman to his hero, Lincoln. But they have seemed to me to be befittingly applicable to the death-efforts of the Captain of Redemption to reach port from the voyage of discovery and salvation for all people who believe.

I revert to the opening sentence of this volume: "As the taut string has its fundamental note, upon which the whole musical gamut is based, so human life must have its fundamental, which becomes a determining factor in all conduct and activities." For not only must there be that fundamental; but in every true Christian life there must be tenseness of nerve, a strain of effort, to reach the harmonies of the universal music of the divine symphony. Flabbiness, laxity, slackness of purpose make a decadent faith. Those who love ease and pleasure will allow the nerves to drop into a state of rest that means deadness to all touch of the great Musician. And the strange paradox follows: those who have sought ease thus, lose all of the real sweetness of the song of humanity.

As the active, alert body may logically be in the path to physical health and prosperity, so the intense soul, in its outlook upon the eternal world, with Christ the great Sacrifice at its center, may be in the orbit of divine perfection.

Chapter XVI

THE GREATEST OF ALL DREAMS

LOOKING through the kaleidoscope of time, the Christian idealist, pointing his instrument toward eternity, beholds configurations of wondrous beauty. He sees temples and landscapes, forests and plains, rivers and oceans which fairly startle him with their glory. Averting his eyes from the vision and looking again upon an everyday world, he is filled with doubt and misgiving. Faith comes to his aid as he again gazes into an eternity which holds for him a charm and interest that ever increases. The land of dreams, the world of visions, the universe of perfection lies before this man of faith, the disciple of the universal Redeemer

When the Christian has reached such a viewpoint, he stands upon the threshold of a new day, at the dawn of a new selfhood. If there are whispering spirits in the air, his ear is unclogged for their message; if the stars have a story to tell, their language is understandable to his heart. As the adolescent youth, at the threshold of manhood, enters a world of unfolding mystery, so does this advancing spirit of the redeemed man approach a country whose every symbol of existence is capable of an infinite realization in consciousness. Great yearnings take hold of the heart; the deeps of mighty seas seem to be broken up; the soul appears to be loosening herself from the moorings of time and the laws of gravitation, and to be taking to herself the wings of the imagination.

The habitat of the soul is henceforth to be the land of vision; and the content of pure being, the invisible entities of God's great, inner world, enters into whatever the liberated spirit would construct. It is a new world, but in it are the essential elements of the old, such as the hopes and yearnings of the earth-born individual on some autumn evening when leaves rustle to the ground in a great woodland. And so, it is a realm where the insoluble questions of time are borne for answer and unfoldment. What is the ultimate end of human struggle, the final resultant of civilizations? Such questions belong to the world which the Christian enters by faith.

What does the Christian carry with him into the realms of faith? Chiefest of all of his instrumentalities of achievement is the key of prayer, the attitude of entreaty. This becomes to him a veritable open-sesame to all of the hidden mysteries of the universe. The bearer of this master-key is to tread the highways of God's thought, to enter all castles and palaces of the King, to explore all treasure-houses where he may view the crown jewels of the Eternal Ruler. The new inhabitant is an explorer, and going afar seeks the corner-stones of all great surveys that the soul has made during creation. Wherever the soul of time-bound man has gone in her cravings for beauty and peace, there the new spirit goes with the power of interpretation. The quest is unceasing, and assuredly, in process of the search, the redeemed soul must come face to face in the new world with King Man. Eternity is God's answer to the soul's craving for self-realization. All of the appalling mystery of time must be torn off as a veil; the craving of the cycles must be realized. For I can conceive of no yearning of the soul greater than this: to know the essential nature of man, and to understand his destiny.

And this self-realization on the part of man is to be accomplished in the light of a new consciousness which recognizes God as a monopolist of all forces, resources, potentialities. The greatest of all days is that eternal day whose dawn brings a flooding of the universe with the knowledge of God. It is to mark the time when "the kingdoms of the world are become the kingdoms of our Lord and His Christ." Man finds himself the possessor of infinite greatness because he is indissolubly linked with the Infinite. The weakness of the race on the shores of time is to be attributed to that appalling selfishness which refuses to make a confidant of God; which is unwilling to take Him into a partnership of thought-life. When the disillusioned soul has entered the new sphere, her eyes will behold a "new Heaven and a new Earth," because the Almighty will be visible, and He ever makes things new to those who recognize Him.

The soul's self-realization is but the cumulative dream-life of the centuries on the part of individuals and nations. Consider the latter: every nation has had its dreams of world-empire, of independence, of a large place in the affairs of the earth. We may consider the present waking China, rubbing her eyes after forty centuries of sleep—but a sleep that has been troubled now and again by dreams. Now, she is arousing herself, and looking with great, wondering eyes out into the country that rose before her in visions of the night. China wants a better religion, better training of the heart, a more practical type of mind-training. So great has been her desire for the best of the universe that she has called upon Christian nations to take their master-key, prayer, and unlock with it the unknown riches of the Ruler of the nations. For China has a feeling that there are great secrets of government, of power, of national glory if she could only get them into the light.

Consider the individual: his dream life is a cumulative inheritance from the ages. It has been handed down, with many adulterations, it is true; but in the complex makeup of each personality there is a rich composite of a long line of personalities reaching into the vague and unknown past. Indeed, they reach back beyond the borders of time, since man traverses an eternal circle which is impinged upon by the planet on which he lives. If he has much to look forward to it is only because he has much to which he can look back. He has a great future because he has had a great past. His riches in the unexplored future are without computation because no calculus could enumerate the priceless values that lie in the background of his origin. The very vagueness of his concept of himself in his beginnings is attributable to the vastness of the world in which he was born. He has traveled so far that he has lost count of the mile-posts along the road. And altho he is covered with dust and grime, he is a royal traveler still, and has his face turned toward kingship in the end.

It must ever be borne in mind, however, that this kingship is attainable only on the fundamental hypothesis of essential unity. Man, by linking himself to God has all things; isolating himself he loses all. All that he has lost in the past has resulted through his selfish ambition to separate his kingdom from the Kingdom of God. By striving to place the crown upon his own brow, as an independent sovereign, he has been rebuked by divine law, becoming a slave to low passions and ideals as a logical result. His empire, so established in arrogancy, has had within itself certain weak and temporal elements which have brought pain and vexation. He has tried in vain, as independent pretender to the crown, to solve the riddle of his destiny, but all answers that have come to him have been filled with the doubtful meaning of the Delphic oracle. He has gone into the laboratory of time, and there, with his test-tubes, his mortar and pestle, has striven to find out the inner meaning of the elements. He has entered the operating room of science and with keen scalpel has dissected the physical dwelling of the soul in the vain hope that he might understand himself. He has delved in the great libraries of all nations, deciphering many hieroglyphics and strange symbols, striving thereby to get some clue to the hidden path along which the spirit of man has come. But in his every quest, man has been disappointed, and in the end, heartbroken. Looking out into the Stygian blackness of eternity he has cried inquiring,

> "Is there, is there balm in Gilead?
> Tell me, tell me, I implore,"

only to hear the hollow echo of the black raven of mystery,

> "Never-more, never-more!"

It is from the despair of such a hopeless quest that man has looked toward the gleam of a new light that shimmers in the skies. He turns, as Galileo, from an effete, geocentric system to the living, heliocentric philosophy. Formerly, the center of his faith and hope was himself; the new center is God. And the change works a revolution in his thought equal to that which came to medieval scientists when they changed from earth to sun as center of the system of planets in which we are working out our destiny.

The God whom the Hebrews knew and honored, the Jehovah of Sinai, alone, can interpret to the race the mysterious dream-life of the soul, the perplexing riddle of existence. Through Him, there comes a wondrous peace, a calm serenity, as the vexed heart considers the vastness of the surrounding universe. For the divide of death itself becomes to man, trusting in God, an invisible boundary line, like that existing between two countries, and used only for convenience. In reality, the whole globe is one extended sphere; likewise, the entire universe to the man of faith is extended from one center, namely, God. And whoever would have a co-rulership with Him over all that exists must stand at the center! Only from that point can he reasonably hope to have a share in the wielding of that centralized power which shapes the courses of the stars.

The Son of Man is the interpreter of life. He does not consider physical death an abiding fact, a fundamental reality. "I am the resurrection and the life; he that believeth in me, tho he were dead, yet shall he live." This expression certainly declares death to be nothing more than a logical accident. Jesus recognizes it as one of those sad circumstances that must accompany development. But His is a new and unique interpretation of death in that only life-terms are used. His definition of life crushes all ideals and concepts; the great and eternal "I," representing an undying personality, is connotative of nothing excepting vital, living forces. Death is a part of a process, and as such is indispensable to God's scheme of unfoldment. And through this process Jesus declares all life must be drawn. Death may be represented as a mortar into which all elements, belonging to man, are thrown. Many a precious image is gathered there, only to be crusht to atoms by the cruel pestle, for Jesus is the most relentless iconoclast of history. And some sweet, tender plants out of the scented gardens of the heart are to be crusht into an unrecognizable pulp. Why? That a life may spring up out of the dust, constructed according to the will of God. All knowledge, art, science, are useful; but they must be broken into an atomic mass by the pestle of this divine Will. Riches, knowledge, culture are of value, but not within themselves; only as they can be grounded into dust are they capable of becoming a fine composite, beautifying the soul. Education becomes of value to the mind just as the cocoon is of value to the chrysalis. But tho the cocoon be of finest silk, it must be utterly thrown aside;

yet, the released butterfly, fluttering away into the upper air, carries with it whatever of essential value lay in the finely woven strands that were wound about it in its embryonic state.

The whole creation, in Pauline language, is groaning for deliverance. And this groaning is but the language of the suffering that must ever come from the mortar-and-pestle process subjecting all things to the Will as a constructive personality. The real crux of all suffering arises from the unwillingness of sentient beings to come into line with the purpose of God.

But when this alignment of two wills has been achieved, the greatest of all events in man's history transpires; the will of man complying with the will of God takes every broken fragment of old idols and ideals of time and constructs with them a new temple, "a house not made with hands, eternal in the heavens." Roses that have been crusht in the mortar become amaranthine, and ever adorn the palace; plants that have been ground into ashes, spring into a new life by some crystal river and ever bear leaves for the healing of the nations. The soul-house is best adorned of all temples, since it represents the resultant of the suffering spirit of humanity and the suffering Spirit of God for untold ages.

I have spoken of the soul's final estate as being represented by a temple, and I can think of no figure that more befittingly illustrates man's spiritual condition in time or eternity. The soul may be a temple, beautiful, exquisite, and yet lacking in orderliness, and destitute of the great adornment, namely, spiritual life. For it is quite possible to have the most perfect specimens of art and statuary throughout the splendid structure; to have every corridor and gallery lined with paintings of the masters, and yet to be barren of Spirit. Can any building be more desolate than the empty fane, where He is not? But the temple of eternal beauty is that which has all that art and science can give to perfect and beautify, and which bears the marks of the divine touch, showing that the eternal Will has placed everything where it ought to be. And then at the temple's altar, in the Holy of Holies, there kneels the spirit of the temple itself, in lowly recognition of the Will of the universe. The immortal self of man is thus related to God.